MW01601174

Windfall

JO HERSHBERGER

DENVER, COLORADO

Outskirts Press, Inc.
http://www.outskirtspress.com

ISBN: 978-1-4787-2852-8

Outskirts Press and the "OP" logo are trademarks belonging to Outskirts Press, Inc.

PRINTED IN THE UNITED STATES OF AMERICA

"Life contains but two tragedies. One is not to get your heart's desire; the other is to get it."

—Socrates

This book is dedicated to Dick and our family
for their support and encouragement

—and to the readers of *Some Good Memory*
who begged to know more about Doris.

Acknowledgments

I am indebted to all those who provided me with valuable insight and information during the journey.

They include Katie Neuser, Laura Pascual, Karl Hershberger, Paul Hershberger, Ann Tudor, Martha Jeffers, Dr. Robert E. Clemency Jr., Linda Krzyzaniak, Kenny Carta, and the staffs at MarineMax in Fort Myers, FL, East Chicago (IN) Marina, Walt Williams Insurance in Steger, IL, and Whiteman-Cook Greenhouses in Plymouth, IN.

Prologue

2005

Doris

April

"I don't think I'll ever get over this." Doris Lochschmidt sighed heavily and glanced around the kitchen table at her three old friends. "I've never been so lonesome in all my life."

Mechanically, she trudged across the room and picked up the coffee pot. Through the crack in the open window over her sink she caught a whiff of the earth as it softened under an all-day drizzle. She paused, distracted by the buds on the lilac bush beside her clothesline pole. Had they plumped out since the day before?

"Sit down." Rosie's voice was kind but firm. "Geez, we didn't come to your place to be waited on."

Doris obeyed, just as she always had when she'd become friends with Rosie, Kate, and Cheryl in seventh grade—more years ago than she liked to admit. Rosie had been their ringleader back then, always creating the fun and mischief that had bound them together. Now that Rosie had returned to Illinois after a long absence and lived about forty miles north of Rockwell, the two stayed in close touch.

"That's right." Sweet Cheryl covered Doris' hand with her own. "We came to see if we could help. Lordy, hon, it doesn't matter if you live here in Rockwell or Chicago, like me. When the love of your life dies, you fall into this huge empty hole. Every single day." Blinking back tears, Cheryl added, "I know. I've been there."

Although she realized that Cheryl had been in her shoes and meant well, Doris nodded appreciatively and withdrew her hand.

"That's why we waited for ten days . . . I wanted to drive down from South Bend for Alan's funeral, but . . ." Kate, the writer, tucked a few strands of salt-and-pepper hair behind her ear as she struggled to find words. "We—we agreed it would be better if we came after all the hubbub was over."

Doris was touched that her friends were taking Alan's death so hard but damn, she thought, I'd rather be tryin' to make someone else feel better than be the one that everyone's fussin' over.

As they sat quietly, she recalled the day three years ago when the four of them had met for the first time in more than fifty years. They'd had a strained, awkward lunch at her restaurant, The Boulder, before they'd been able to recapture their old camaraderie in the sunny blue-and-yellow kitchen where Doris and her sister, Violet, still created some of the town's best catered meals. At that time, however, it had been Doris who'd been in charge. She'd asked Cheryl and Kate to help her rescue Rosie, who was grieving herself to death over the losses of her husband and her mother.

It had worked, Doris realized now as she nibbled around

the edge of her cookie. Since that time, Rosie had bought a nice little condo in Bourbonnais, had taken a parttime job at Walmart, and still played a vital role in the continuing art education of Colton Powers, the boy she'd tutored the last ten years.

Shaking her head to rein in her wandering thoughts, Doris remembered how three years ago they'd all promised to get together on a regular basis. They'd planned to meet downtown in Chicago and talked about a day in South Bend, where Kate could show them around Notre Dame. But somehow they always ended up back in Rockwell. They'd have lunch at The Boulder, drive around town to revisit their old haunts, and end up at Doris' kitchen table, where they'd drink coffee, eat her oatmeal raisin cookies, and share laughs. Lots of laughs.

It didn't seem to matter that Cheryl was now a well-known Chicago singer and president of the Wish List Auxiliary Board at Children's Memorial Hospital. And it didn't mean a thing that Kate was a famous author of children's books and had important things to do. They always left their successes at home the way a locust sheds his shell, and came right back to their roots.

Doris smiled wanly as she studied her three friends. They'd all had their troubles. Cheryl had weathered the loss of her beloved husband and profoundly retarded son. Now it was Kate whose deep worry lines reflected the stress of dealing with her husband's early stages of Parkinson's. Still, Doris knew that her friends would help her get through Alan's death.

"So, d'ya wanta ride our bikes to the cemetery?" Trying

to pump a little lame humor into the group, she referred to their first experience together when, as seventh-graders pedaling on the cemetery road, they'd been chased by two hobos. After she and her friends had stumbled into Rosie's house breathless and frightened, they'd solemnly vowed never to tell a soul about their scare. That experience and their pledge to silence had forged a solid friendship that had weathered all these years.

"Naw, my bike's too old," Rosie chuckled, passing the plate of cookies around the table. "And the first minute we hear that <u>any</u> of us has told <u>anyone</u> about those hobos is the day we'll know one of us is ready for assisted living!"

They all laughed in agreement.

"You know, Doris, every time I eat one of these I think of the day I drove out to the farm where you and Bill lived." Kate selected two golden brown cookies. "I was home from Butler for Christmas break, and there you were—married with four kids already."

"And two more to go," Doris reminded her.

"I felt like a child myself that day and wondered if I was wasting my time studying journalism. You seemed to have it all." Kate shook her head at the memory.

"And <u>I</u> felt like a frump in my housedress and white socks. Oh my God, what a mess I was then!" Doris had never told Kate how embarrassed <u>she'd</u> been to be caught in a shabby house with three wild kids and a squalling infant. At least Bill hadn't been home that afternoon to berate her in front of her friend.

"We all had our days, didn't we?" Cheryl swished her well-cut hair as she glanced around the table. "Lordy, I married the North Shore's most eligible bachelor and found out he was a drunk and a womanizer. Then I fell for that good-for-nothing drummer in the band I was singing with and found out he liked pot and credit cards." Sipping her coffee, she reflected. "If Jarvis hadn't come along and swept me off my feet, I'd probably be in a homeless shelter by now. But still singing," she added, her brown eyes dancing.

"Yeah, and I know I'll make it through this, too," Doris affirmed. "Hey, there's some pictures we used at the funeral home you'd probably like to see. I'll get 'em."

While Cheryl refilled the coffee cups, Doris spread out a group of photos that ranged from black-and-white to grainy color to clear digital productions. They murmured as they viewed the pictures of Alan with her older brothers, Vic and Charley Panczyk, and spoke again of the shot that had made Alan a local basketball legend and propelled Rockwell to its first-ever state tourney.

"That was when we were in eighth grade, and our world revolved around basketball," Kate recalled. "The whole town worshiped the boys on that team."

"Me 'n Alan used to talk basketball a lot. I'd take meals over to his house after his wife got so sick with kidney failure. She'd always brighten right up when we'd tell her about how Charley and him made such a great team. She especially liked this picture," Doris added, showing them the photo of Charley firing a pass to Alan under the basket.

"Later, after she died, he became my best friend, my lover, and my go-to guy for everything. He was so damn much fun!" She could feel the tears coming. "How could he just drop dead like that? Without no warning at all?"

As she glanced through the pictures, she told them again of how Alan had died at his desk at Atwater Construction. Her sons, Doug and Dirk who'd worked for Alan ever since they'd been in high school, had found him slumped over his paperwork and had "cried like babies" when they helped carry his casket to the hearse.

"Oh, hon, I wish we could make it better for you." Cheryl's eyes were moist.

"Sometimes," Kate said, her cup and saucer clattering as she lifted them from the table, "there just aren't any words, are there?" Placing her dishes in the sink, she threw her arms around Doris, who made no attempt to break away. Kate was so right. A genuine hug sure beat a bunch of gibberish.

She led her friends into the living room. There, as they settled in comfortably, she found the energy to bring them up to date on all six of her children and reminded them that she and her eldest, Denny, remained estranged.

"He still lives on the farm where me 'n Bill were. He's wore out three wives—but never had no kids. Always blamed me for leavin' his dad when he was ten." She paused. "Come to think of it, he did send me a little sympathy card from the Dollar General a few days after Alan . . ."

She stopped for a moment to compose herself.

"But Doug and Dirk?" Cheryl still seemed concerned about the two who were so close to Alan. "Will they stay on with Atwater Construction?"

"Good question." Doris herself wondered. "You never saw two more different brothers in your life. Well, maybe except Cain and Abel." She straightened the magazines on the coffee table. "Doug, the one Bill always called 'Grumpy' 'cause of his temper, is such a party boy. All he wants to do is have fun. But he's married again and got himself a really good wife."

"And Dirk?" She thought about her youngest child before she spoke. "You talk about the word 'focus' and he's it. I s'pose he always hated it that Bill called him 'Runt' 'cause he was such a scrawny little guy. But him and Nora have two nice boys. He's a planner, that one." She looked at her friends. "Dirk'll come out all right. That much I'm sure of."

"I've gotta get going," Rosie broke in. "Colton's coming over for supper tonight and I need to pick up groceries. Geez," she added as she looked out the window, "it's starting to clear up. I sure hope the lilacs don't get nipped. It's supposed to freeze tonight."

After they gathered their belongings, they paused at the door to discuss a place for another get-together.

"Do come to Chicago." Cheryl flipped her dark hair over her collar.

"We always say that." Rosie laughed. "But we always end up here."

"You decide where," Kate told Doris. "But in the meantime, email us about Doug and Dirk. We want to make sure they're okay."

"I think—I hope they will be," Doris assured them. Embracing each one, she told them again that she was the luckiest person in the world to have friends like them.

After she closed the door behind them, she pulled out the basket stuffed with sympathy cards. In the middle of the stack she found the one she was looking for—the cheap, slightly perfumed paper with the bright red rose and rhymed message that even she recognized as corny.

"Denny," it was signed. Not "Love, Denny." Just "Denny."

She placed it on top, wishing with all her heart that he were at her kitchen table so that she could make her firstborn child a cup of coffee. She only hoped to God her other five kids wouldn't heap any more troubles on her already-full plate.

Spring

2005

Doug

April

A stiff spring breeze tugged at the envelopes in Doug Lochschmidt's fist and heightened the restlessness that stirred in his chest as he stepped out of the Rockwell Post Office. He tossed the junk mail into a nearby trash container, keeping only two bills and his May issue of *NASCAR Illustrated*—hardly worth his time and effort to pick up. As he headed for his two-year-old red Grand Prix, he heard the screech of a car as it zipped into the parking place down the street.

"Hey, dude!"

Doug grinned. He might have known. Springing from a sleek black Mustang and jogging toward him was Nick Rigoni, still looking as fit as he'd been when they played high-school basketball together years ago. His curly black hair shone almost blue in the sunshine.

"Where you been?" Nick groused. "I tried your cell, but you didn't pick up."

Doug shrugged as they exchanged high fives.

"Yeah, gotta recharge it. What's going on?" After hanging out with Nick for most of his fifty years, he still never knew what to expect.

"Hey, I just talked with the guy at the marina in Danville. He's gonna put my boat in tomorrow, so we can cruise around the lake on Saturday." Nick's brown eyes sparkled like a seven-year-old with a new bike. "You up for it?"

Lifting his Daytona 500 cap, Doug scratched his head.

"What time? I promised Maria I'd take her to Applebee's and to see 'Sahara'."

"The two of you could come over and watch something in my home theater," Nick suggested. "I'll be working and you'd have the place to yourselves."

"Thanks anyway." Doug shook his head. "Maria's kinda got the hots for Matthew McConaughey."

"Well, look who's the boss at your house," Nick snickered. "You never had to ask permission to do anything when you were married to Tonya."

"I never cared that much," Doug answered evenly. "I'll go to the lake with you if we're back by four. Otherwise, find someone else. You know Maria and me. We've got something special."

"Yep," Nick conceded, "and I wouldn't mess with that. Anyone who can go to his granddaughter's special day at school and end up marrying the kindergarten teacher is one lucky dude." He jingled his keys and squinted into the sun at Doug. "You've never been one to waste any time making a decision, but that one tops 'em all."

"Don't you forget it." Doug punched Nick playfully on the arm. "Let me know what time Saturday—and thanks."

Before he could turn the key in his ignition, he heard the Mustang's roar and sighed as Nick sped toward Rigoni's Uptown Tap, his family-owned bar that had been a Rockwell institution even before the two of them were born. Doug knew he'd never have a set of wheels like that.

Driving toward the sprawling lumber yard that served as the offices for Atwater Construction, he reflected on Nick's comment. It was true, he realized. He might not have the fancy stuff he dreamed about, but he <u>was</u> one lucky dude!

He felt like a fish out of water this time last year when he first mingled with the old folks at Cherisse's Grandparents' Day at Sweet Briar Elementary, but he'd promised to be there for his granddaughter. After all, Tonya had no interest in attending any event that might classify her as a grandmother.

He perched himself awkwardly on a little wooden chair, sipping apple juice from a paper cup and munching a doughnut with sprinkles, while Cherisse's teacher, Maria Morris, described an average day in kindergarten. Damn, he thought to himself, this little blond is way too cute to be a schoolteacher!

After the presentation, he made a point of talking with Miss Morris, whose blue eyes glowed as she told him that Cherisse was one of the brightest in her group.

"Everyone calls her the NASCAR Queen," she'd confided. "She's the only one in the class who knows that Kevin Harvick wears Number 29 and Ryan Newcomer 39." Her dimples had deepened as she'd smiled up at him.

Erupting in laughter, he slapped his leg and sloshed juice all over the floor. When Miss Morris helped him mop it up with paper towels, he noticed her ring finger was empty.

"You like NASCAR?" He couldn't believe a school-teacher might know something about his favorite sport.

"You bet!" She dumped the pile of soggy towels into a wastebasket.

Suddenly, he felt shy, like a kindergartner himself, as he realized they'd made a connection.

"Could I . . .Would you mind if—well, if I called you sometime?"

"Gramps, your face is all red," Cherisse blurted as she swished her black pony tail and tugged on his hand.

"That'd be nice," Maria Morris answered, gazing directly into his eyes.

"Your face is red too, Miss Morris," Cherisse observed. "Are the two of you getting a fever?"

Recalling that life-changing moment in the classroom helped ease some of the dread that Doug had felt each time he reported for work since Alan's death two weeks earlier. Thank God for Maria, he thought as he guided his truck into a slot near the end of Atwater's back lot.

He'd wondered if he'd met his soul mate the first time the two of them split an order of onion rings at The Boulder shortly after Grandparents' Day. Later that evening his feelings were confirmed when she playfully called him "kochany."

"Where'd you hear that?" Stunned, he sat up straight on the sofa in her little apartment.

"It's just a Polish expression for someone dear to you." It was then she confessed she'd been born Maria Mrozinski to a Polish couple on the southwest side of Chicago. "But I changed my name to Maria Morris when I started performing on stage. Some of the little summer theaters where I worked didn't have enough room on their marquees for Mrozinski. I just kept 'Morris' when I got a real job."

"But <u>my</u> mom used to call me 'kochany' when I was little," he replied, adding that his mother's family name was Panczyk. "She was from a big Polish family."

Maria cocked her head. "There used to be a terrific pianist named Tommy Panczyk in New York."

"Yep. My Uncle Tommy. Mom's brother."

"Get out!" She pushed him so hard that he landed on the floor. "I've traveled all over the world and look at me—I've still taken up with a Polish chlop!" She hugged him, then drew back to take a closer look. "And Tommy Panczyk's nephew. Unbelievable!"

Her playful mood had changed, however, when he asked why she'd stopped performing. As she glanced away, her mouth tightened at the corners and she began wrapping one end of her silk scarf around her fingers.

"My mom and dad were so proud of me. They'd seen me in every production I'd ever been in since I was a little girl. So when I got the role of Luisa in 'The Fantasticks,' they headed straight to New York."

Doug hadn't a clue who the hell Luisa was, but sensed it best not to utter a word as he waited until she could continue.

"The van bringing them in from LaGuardia was in a terrible accident and I lost them both. I didn't perform that night and never set foot on stage again." She shook her head as if to chase the memory. "Too painful," she sighed.

Doug took her hands in his and brushed them with his lips.

"A team of counselors and a perceptive priest pulled me through it." When she gazed directly at him, he saw the deep pain that had surfaced in her blue eyes. Feeling a lump rising in his throat, he tried to imagine life without his own mom.

"I should tell you," she warned, "sometimes a freaky little thing can set me off, like a song from 'The Fantasticks', and I go into a deep funk. It—it's a scar I have to live with."

God, he wished he was good with words! Instead, he whispered, "Like I'm Mr. Perfect myself."

He longed to show more wisdom that evening, but somehow she accepted him, too.

A few weeks later after school was out, they were married, and he never stopped marveling that under her buttoned-up schoolmarm exterior lay the sexiest woman he'd ever encountered.

That next Saturday, Doug could feel the dark cloud of Alan's death lifting as he climbed into Nick's speedboat and ran his fingers over the soft, cream-colored seats with burgundy piping. Knowing that he and Maria had a movie date followed by who-knew-what-else that night made him feel like a high-school senior again. He untied the back ropes at the pier, while Nick took care of the front, then slid into his seat. The gurgle of the inboard motor as they moved away from the dock assured him that this first ride of the season would be one of the best.

He was not disappointed when Nick opened it up and they flew across Lake Vermilion. The smell of fuel and water, coupled with the cool bite of the early spring air, chased away his emptiness.

He'd barely been able to get through the last two weeks at work since his younger brother, Dirk, had found Alan collapsed at his desk. So far, he felt that Pete Nolan, the general manager, would keep both of them on, but they hadn't talked about it.

Maria was helping him deal with his grief, just as she had with the bag of regret he'd carried around with him for the last twenty-five years after he'd had to marry his high-school sweetheart. The sharp-tongued, free-spending Tonya had given him two daughters–Cherisse's unpredictable mom Renee, and Ramona, who now lived in Montana with her husband, Devin Gregg, and son, Dakota.

With Maria at his side, he felt headed in the right direction. Still–he bit his lip as they hit a large wave–he'd give anything to have a boat like this. Or a flashy car. Or a brand new Harley. He turned and let the mist spray across his face, trying to ignore the envy that bounced around in his chest like a pinball being flung from flipper to flipper.

"Hey, I'm gonna haul this thing up to Lake Michigan in a coupla weeks!" Nick shouted over the slap of the waves. "Wanna go along?"

"You know me." He gave Nick a thumbs up.

They cruised the lake several times, checking out the progress on two new homes and the spots where they liked to fish after the waters warmed. Eventually, Nick cut his speed, idled up to the marina pier and announced, "Time for a burger and a beer."

They knotted their ropes around the posts and ambled

toward the small restaurant attached to the showroom.

As Doug smeared catsup and mustard on his bun and chomped into his sandwich, he mumbled, "This food's okay, but nothing's as good as a beer at your place or a burger down at Mom's Boulder."

Nick lifted his bottle and took a long swig.

"How's your mom doing anyway?" Doug could feel Nick's eyes boring into him. "I mean I gotta tell you, dude, that you've looked like you been on a real bender for the last coupla weeks. I can't imagine what Alan's death is doing to her."

Doug examined the singed edges of his burger so Nick couldn't see the tears that threatened to give him away. "She's a little better since her old friends came to see her a few days ago. We've all told her to take some time off, but you know Mom. She's gotta be down at The Boulder, even though Darcy and her girls practically run the place."

"Yep, just like my Uncle Danny. He practically lived at the bar until Aunt Colleen made him retire and move to Florida." Nick finished his burger and eyed the remainder of Doug's. "I was lucky he made it easy for me to buy into the business before I could blow everything on cars and girls. You gonna finish that?"

"Naw, I'm not that hungry." Doug pushed the plate aside, wishing Nick would change the subject. "Let's go look at the new boats before we take another spin."

As he and Nick strolled into the showroom, Doug felt the familiar sensation of awe. He whistled softly at the sight of two pontoons, a deck boat, two inboard-outboards, and a couple of shiny silver-colored fishing boats, all waiting to be hauled away by the guy who had enough money to buy any of them. He was surprised when Nick paused at the first pontoon, a sensible boat he knew his buddy would never consider.

"You coulda gone in with your mom at The Boulder. Prob'ly." Never looking up, Nick pretended to be interested in the pontoon.

Doug groaned inwardly. Obviously his buddy wasn't finished talking about the choices they'd made in their younger days. He checked the price tag on the pontoon–reasonable enough but boring as hell—before he answered.

"That was never on the table. Alan put me 'n Dirk to work at his place before we ever had a chance to think about anything else. You remember that." He inched closer to the deck boat. A guy could have some fun in that and still be able to cart several friends around, he reasoned.

"Well, Alan sure was a great—kinda like a dad to you. I mean, your dad–"

"Shit, my dad never called me anything but 'Grumpy'," he shot back. Doug clamped his teeth to keep the muscle in his right cheek from throbbing the way it always did when he was upset. "If it hadn't been for Alan, I'd be lucky to be washing dishes somewhere today. And, of course, Spud–"

"Now that was some dude!" Nick chuckled, lightening up. "Spud the Garbageman. More like Spud the Wise Man. He taught us more stuff than we ever learned in school."

"He sure showed me how to control my temper—got me that punching bag and told me to smash the shit out of it when I was just a kid." Doug rubbed his chin. "You know what though? No one ever called me 'Grumpy' again. Well, except Denny."

"It's kind of like you had two dads but neither one was your own. Know what I mean?" Nick climbed the three-step ladder to inspect the interior of the larger speedboat.

"And Uncle Charley. Don't ever forget Uncle Charley. He's the one who coached me—showed me how to copy his corner shot and play defense." He eyed the price tag and wondered who would ever buy this one. "Make that three dads, I guess."

"Aw, you'd prob'ly have gone pro if you hadn't hooked up with old hot-pants Tonya. We made a pretty good team— you and me. Racked up a bunch of wins, too!" Nick patted the side of the boat as he stepped off the ladder. "Nice tub, but an awful lot of horsepower for this lake."

Doug wandered over to check the cost of the fishing boats. Maybe someday, after he and Maria had finished their remodeling, he could afford one of these.

"Damn! We sound like a couple of old farts," he said. While he liked to kick around memories with Nick, he often felt a sense of loss. He thought of Nick's boat, his new home, and his ability to snag any girl he wanted, then recalled his own wasted years with Tonya.

With her black hair and blue eyes, she'd been the cheer-leader all the guys had coveted—and yet she'd chosen him. Some prize! The sassy edge that had made her so cute in high school had transformed into nothing but bitchiness after they'd married at twenty. Diapers, crying babies, and messy kitchens had only made her worse.

Doug plunked down some bills for lunch and left them on the table, then zipped his windbreaker as he and Nick wandered out of the showroom. There was more winter chill in the April air than he'd realized.

"Another loop around the lake before we head home?" he asked Nick.

Doug felt his cloud of dissatisfaction fade when Nick parked in front of the rambling old home at the edge of town that he and Maria were remodeling. Not even his well-off good-looking friend had someone like Maria waiting for him.

Jogging up the splintered steps, he sniffed a clean aroma as he opened the door and heard her singing along to the cast recording of "Ragtime." As soon as he entered the kitchen, he realized she'd papered the section of walls above the tops of their cupboards.

"Be down in a minute." She remained focused on smoothing air bubbles out of the last strip. "Gotta get these two pieces to match up just right." Pressing a roller over the seam, she checked it and climbed down. "How's the lake?"

He hugged her and kissed the end of her nose, right next to a white spot of paste.

"I would've helped you with this," he scolded. "Makes me feel like a bum to be out cruising the lake with Nick while you're home slaving away."

"You know I love decorating." She gave him a squeeze and began to clean up the scraps. "You and I are good at a lot of things together, but wallpapering's not one of them."

Lifting the lid on their cookie jar, he pulled out a handful of Double Stuffs. He thought twice and put all but one back. Either Maria had been shrinking his jeans in the laundry or he'd added an inch to his waistline this last winter.

"That border looks great." He was amazed how a few pictures of bird houses and seed packets could brighten up their aging kitchen. "I'll bring home some paint next week—yeah, you can pick the color." He grinned. "I can probably do the walls on Saturday."

She picked up a notepad from the counter. "You had three calls—one from your mom right after you left. She wanted us to come over this evening, but I told her we were busy and we'd see her tomorrow. Also, Renee wondered if we could keep Cherisse tonight, but I explained that we had a commitment. She said she'd ask a girlfriend who owes her a favor. I don't think she was very happy about it though."

"Well, I don't like her dropping off Cherisse like a stray pup either."

It seemed to him that Renee had been yanking his chain more than ever lately, using Cherisse as her bait. He'd never been able to trust Renee—his own daughter, for God's sake—since his mom had fired her after she'd "borrowed" restaurant items from the back room as a teenage waitress at The Boulder.

Then, halfway through her senior year, Renee had given birth to Cherrise after a short fling with a married drug rep who came to town once a month. Now, a single mom, she struggled to pay the rent on a shabby apartment over the hardware store, as she flitted from job to job. She sure would've made a good con artist, he reflected ruefully. He couldn't begin to count the times he'd allowed her to extract money from him, like he was a walking ATM.

"And this third call?" He scowled as he read Maria's note. "What the hell? Bennett Priddy, the stuffy banker? Called me? On a Saturday?" He crumpled the paper and threw it down on the wooden kitchen table.

"Oh, he was very nice—just said he needed to meet with you in his office on Monday morning at ten." Maria grabbed the bucket of glue and headed toward the garage.

"Damn!" He pounded the table. "Probably found a two-cent mistake in my account."

"Oh, sweetie, don't get all hyper over it. You don't even know what he wants." She patted his arm. "I'm going to shower and get ready to go out."

Nodding glumly, he reached for another cookie. He knew he hadn't missed a car payment. But he never had liked that guy. Even back in high school. Priddy could've led their basketball team to state if he'd been able to manage his 6'6" frame. Instead, he'd always dribbled the ball before a shot, allowing his opponent to make an easy steal. He'd been the top gun in student government and never missed being on the honor roll. But to Doug's way of thinking, Priddy was no fun at all.

He wiped the cookie crumbs from his mouth and took a deep breath, resolving not to let the prospect of a meeting with this nerd ruin his night with Maria.

Dirk

A few blocks away, Dirk Lochschmidt had a similar thought as he spaded his garden: Wonder why ol' Ben left that message on our machine?

He'd gone into the house for a bottle of water and pushed the button when he found the phone blinking. His golfing partner wanted to see him in his office at the bank at ten on Monday. Ben didn't say why, but Dirk figured he wanted to tweak their men's summer league schedule.

He hoped it would be okay for him to leave his book-keeping job at Atwater's to run to the bank for a few minutes. Dirk knew Alan wouldn't have cared, but he wasn't so certain about Pete Nolan. The business sure had been stirred up since Alan had dropped dead on them. Well, he thought, he'd make up the time if Pete insisted. A short conversation about golf with Ben would be a welcome change after so many days of sadness and uncertainty.

He checked his watch. Nora and their sons should be back from Danville in an hour or so. He'd told her he'd pass on the opportunity to shop for jeans and summer shoes for the boys. After all, this was the weekend he'd been waiting for all winter. The seeds he'd ordered when there'd been fourteen inches of snow on the ground were lined up in their bulk packets against the wheelbarrow—two kinds of lettuce, spinach, red radishes, and carrots. Just the sight of them lifted his spirits

Nearby, in the freshly turned earth, a robin tugged a long worm from the soil. Spaghetti for lunch, Dirk thought, remembering Spud Zylstra's old comment every spring. Dirk had always been grateful to his uncle for showing him the joys of gardening. It had been a project that he could do on his own—something that had transformed him from the useless "Runt," as his dad always called him, to a worthy provider for his mom, his siblings, Uncle Spud, and Aunt Violet.

He savored every aspect of gardening, starting with the chart he designed on graph paper each winter, the rows neatly marked in colored pencil and enough free space at the corners for Nora's nasturtiums and marigolds. Today's first planting, he thought, might be his favorite of the whole season, but he also looked forward to hoeing the tender seedlings, placing old newspapers between the rows to discourage weeds, and then harvesting the bounty that started with the leaf lettuce and extended into late October with the fat orange pumpkins and golden squash.

As he tied string between sticks to mark his rows, he couldn't help but indulge in the pride that washed over him each summer when people around Rockwell told him he had the prettiest garden in town. Sometimes even Nora came home from the secretary's job she'd held at the grain elevator for twenty-five years with a compliment for him.

Last fall her green eyes had glowed when she told him

that a local farmer who'd delivered a load of corn to the elevator mentioned that he'd driven by their place just to admire the garden.

"Not bad for a couple of townies." She'd grinned, her auburn hair brushing his cheek as she gave him a hug.

Sprinkling carrot seeds in a shallow groove, he covered them gently and speculated that maybe he should have been a farmer himself. Nope–he rejected that thought the minute it formed–I'd never want to be like my dad and Denny. Neither of them, he recalled, was a planner. A planter, yes. A planner, no. There was a heckuva difference.

He breathed deeply, inhaling the sweet air and its promise of hope. If only, he thought as he dropped the lettuce seeds into the ground, I could get this same kick out of my work. I'm sick of doing books in someone else's office. I'd just like something to call my own.

Like that's gonna happen, he muttered. As the tail end of Bill and Doris Lochschmidt's brood of six, he'd always been last in line for outgrown clothes, patched-up toys, and dribs of food passed around the table.

"You're the littlest. You're always gonna suck hind tit." His dad had taunted him with those words so often he would have believed them—if it hadn't been for Spud and Alan Atwater.

The crunch of tires on the gravel driveway interrupted his thoughts.

"Dad!" Holding up a new catcher's mitt, fourteen-year-old Carter sprang from the aging blue Corolla before Nora turned off the engine. "Look what Mom bought me!" His gray eyes sparkled as he swept his sandy hair out of his eyes.

Dirk wiped his hands on his jeans. "Seems like maybe she should have gotten you a haircut," he observed. "Nice glove, though."

"If I'm gonna be the JV catcher this year, I've gotta have a decent glove right now." Carter pounded his fist in the center. "I can always get a haircut."

Dirk rumpled his son's hair affectionately. We need to put some meat on his bones, he thought, or some of those muscle-bound base runners are going to destroy him at home plate.

"Dad! Dad!" Twelve-year-old Logan scrambled out of the back seat, waving a package. "I got a Lego NASCAR set!"

Dirk took a second look at his dark-haired son. The kid must have grown since he left home this morning. It was becoming a real challenge to keep him in clothes.

"I thought you went for jeans and shoes." He glanced at Logan's kit and gave Nora a straight look that implied, How much did you spend anyway.

In the bright sunshine, he was surprised to notice that Nora's once-fiery red hair was fading and now frosted with gray. Still athletic and exactly his height, she gave him a playful punch and looked him in the eye.

"They had such great sales today that I got the jeans and shoes and still had money left over. I thought we oughtta reward the guys for making the honor roll." She set her bundles on the cement slab near the back steps and surveyed the garden. "Looks like you got a lot done this morning. It'll make for good eating! Thanks, honey."

"Hope you didn't plant any carrots." Logan voiced his

annual disdain for vegetables of any kind.

"Already in." Dirk smiled. "You can eat 'em raw or cooked."

"Well, don't waste any space on those Brussels sprouts this year." Carter's nose wrinkled. "They taste like dirt!"

"I'll get those at the nursery in a few days," Dirk answered. "Hardly anybody else grows them. Do you realize how lucky we are?"

"Oh, that reminds me–" Nora studied the plot. "This year I think I'll do something different in the corners." Dirk could tell from her overly-casual attitude that she'd already made a decision. "Lantanas are so showy. We can get a ton of pink and yellow flowers from just a few plants."

"But I'd already figured on zinnias and nasturtiums— and seeds are so much cheaper than plants," he protested. They <u>always</u> highlighted their garden with those two specific flowers. Nora knew that.

"Yeah?" she grinned. "And this from the guy who's practically on his way to invest in Brussels sprout plants. And pepper plants. <u>And</u> tomato plants." She turned to see who was pulling up in another car. "Just pick me up twelve lantanas when you get yours. You gotta believe they'll be spectacular." She shaded her eyes. "Oh, look, guys."

"Grand-do!" Logan shouted, using the pet name Carter had coined as a toddler when he couldn't quite say, "Grandma Doris." He ran to hug her as she emerged from her Lincoln town car. Carter glanced away while he gave her a self-conscious little squeeze.

Dirk loved the classic lines of her seven-year-old gas-guzzler but wished, like Doug, that she'd switch to something with better fuel economy.

"Hey, Mom." Embracing her, he knew his planting time was over but welcomed the intrusion. A hug from his mother brightened any day.

He tried to study her without being obvious. Although she was smiling with the boys, her eyes looked dull and sad. Half an inch of mousy gray now appeared at the roots of her ash-blond hair. When Alan was alive, she'd had a standing appointment with her stylist every Thursday. Now she must have forgotten or just plain didn't care.

"I'm not stayin'," she stated as she stood with her car running and door wide open. "I'm makin' cream pies and wondered if you wanna come over for dessert tonight."

"Yeah!" Logan exclaimed.

"Lemon?" Carter asked.

"One lemon and one coconut." She winked. "Sound good?"

"All right!" Carter shouted.

"Hey, Doris, we'll bring some sloppy joes and baked beans and make it a party," Nora suggested.

"It's a deal." His mom's eyes brightened. "Better make sure there's enough for Violet, too. She's not eatin' too good these days, but sure as we run out, she'll clean up her plate and ask for more."

She took her place behind the wheel and checked her rear view mirror. "See you about 5:30."

Dirk sighed. He'd hoped to watch the White Sox game. Maybe he could still catch the last two or three innings. But he'd also planned on paying for clothes—not extras— for the boys. And he sure as hell had pictured zinnias and nasturtiums at the corners of his garden rather than the lantanas that Nora had ordered. So much for being in charge of his own life. He felt the corners of his mouth tighten.

"She needs us tonight," his wife explained softly. "She and Alan always went out for supper on Saturday nights.

"I know." He sighed as he wondered if the cloud of Alan's death would ever lift.

Windfall

A t precisely 9:45 on Monday morning, Bennett Priddy pulled tight the sheers that covered the large glass wall of his office that faced the lobby. After all, Rockwell bank customers did like to speculate about the conversations that took place behind closed doors and then carry those assumptions to The Boulder for coffee-break fodder with their cronies.

After asking his secretary to hold all his calls, he surveyed the room and decided to straighten the stack of bankers boxes in the corner and tuck the foreclosure file for the video store in his top drawer. All that was left on his desk were two photos of Anne and the kids, his phone and appointment calendar, his prized White Sox baseball signed by Mark Beuhrle, and the folder containing the information he was about to share with the Lochschmidt brothers.

"Anybody home?" There stood his golfing partner, Dirk, ever punctual and neatly dressed, as always, in khaki Dockers, a trim checked shirt, and brown sweater vest.

"C'mon in." He motioned for Dirk to take a chair. "Got

your putter warmed up for next Tuesday?"

As his buddy eased himself into one of the striped wine-and-hunter-green chairs, Ben tried to remember if Dirk had ever been here before. They spent most of their hours together roaming the golf course in a cart. For the first time he realized this buttoned-up guy could pass for a banker in casual clothes.

"You could practice your chipping out there between appointments." Dirk nodded toward the large window and its view of the freshly clipped lawn. "That patch of grass is pretty convenient."

"Wouldn't mind a bit."

Ben's appreciative chuckle was interrupted by a reluctant voice in the doorway.

"Well, I'm here."

Glancing up, Ben tried to keep his professional demeanor from slipping as he spotted Doug. Good lord, this guy, who'd given him grief since they'd been teammates at Rockwell High, must have come straight from the lumber yard. His jeans were speckled with sawdust, and he'd zipped up his windbreaker to cover the ratty t-shirt he usually wore. The sooner Ben could get this maverick in and out of his office, the better. He motioned for him to take the chair next to Dirk.

Doug's face reddened when he realized his brother was in the room. Stiffening himself defensively, he greeted Dirk.

"Hey." Warily, he stationed himself on the edge of the chair as he took in every detail of the well-appointed office.

"Hey, yourself." Dirk's grin was sincere, but his dark eyes revealed his curiosity.

34

"Either of you want any coffee?" Ben's hopes that he could cut the tension with a friendly offer were dashed as he watched them squirm in their chairs. He figured he might as well move on to the reason for the meeting,

"You probably wonder why I asked to see both of you." He settled slowly into his leather chair, brushed his hair from his forehead, and opened the slim file marked "Alan Atwater".

As he turned the pages in the folder, Ben paused to recall his own friendship with Alan and what a great man he had been. He'd taken over the faltering business started by his father, Vince, and converted it into a well-known construction and lumber firm. Alan had always been ready to sharpen his pencil when Lowe's and Menards in Danville threatened to steal his customers. Most of all, he'd been like a dad to these two guys who now sat before him.

Ben smiled at each of them. This definitely was one of the most rewarding moments in any banker's career.

"Alan had a trust with us," he explained. "He left what he felt was an appropriate amount to his sister, Adele, in up-state New York and his son, Arthur, in Washington, D.C. And your mom will never have to worry about money again."

Dirk had turned pale, while Doug was wiping his brow with the sleeve of his jacket. Good lord, Ben reminded himself, he couldn't get derailed by memories of Doug's crazy antics in high school. Clearing his throat, he stressed once more how much Alan had cared for them.

"You'd given him your best since you went to work for him." Again, he pushed the stubborn lock away from his forehead. "He thought of you—whether you realized it or

35

not—as his own sons."

The two sat mutely before him, Dirk still as a statue and Doug wiggling like a preschooler.

"That is why it's my duty—and my pleasure," he added, "to inform you that Alan has remembered you with a sizable amount." He paused, knowing his announcement was about to change their lives.

"Alan Atwater has left each of you two hundred and fifty thousand dollars."

He had expected yelps of joy, but the only sounds in the room came from the battery-powered clock on the wall and a car backfiring on the street. Neither of the brothers had moved a muscle. He wondered if they had heard what he'd said.

Clearing his throat to break the stony silence, he shuffled his documents and advised the two that papers would be drawn up the next day to allow the money to be deposited into either a savings or checking account.

"It's a real windfall for both of you, I know." He shook their hands. Dirk's, he noticed, was cold and clammy, while Doug's was rough and calloused. "Alan's only wish was that you use it wisely, to make better lives for yourselves."

He opened the sheers as the two nodded awkwardly and moved like robots through the lobby. Why, he mused, had this meeting that he'd so eagerly anticipated ended on a flat note? Never before had he delivered good news of such magnitude to people who had been struck so dumb.

I just hope it doesn't affect Dirk's short game, he thought as he began to fill out the forms for distribution.

Doug

Wordless, Doug made a straight line from Priddy's office to his Grand Prix parked behind the bank. Once inside the safety zone of his car, he was ashamed to find his cheeks wet with tears.

Hell, he thought. Priddy said the money could go into "whichever account." I don't even have a savings account and my checking account's running on fumes. He was disgusted with himself for getting choked up. He and Dirk had wept at Alan's funeral, but that was different. Here he was, getting all blubbery over the best damn gift he'd ever received.

His thoughts turned to the man who'd left him all this money. Alan, the real love of his mom's life, who'd always treated her like such a lady. Alan, the guy who along with Spud and Uncle Charley had probably kept him out of reform school during his wild teens. Alan, the boss who'd hired him and helped him develop good work habits and given him a steady income.

Alan. He'd lots rather have the guy himself back at Atwater's than be getting all this cash. He fished around for the little packet of tissues that Maria kept in the glove compartment and went through half of it.

Maria. What would she think? She could stop her redecorating and they could move into a brand new house with a home theater like Nick's. He could pay off his car and buy Cherisse the best bike at Walmart.

One thing was sure: He'd tell Nick before he let Tonya and his daughters in on his news. He chuckled to himself as he pictured his old pal giving a wild whoop and making him buy a round of drinks for everyone at Rigoni's.

And his older sister, Debbie. He'd call her tonight. Even though she had become a successful businesswoman in Champaign, she was still the sib who was his best friend. She'd be thrilled.

But first of all, he needed to tell Mom. As he pulled out of the parking lot at the back of the bank, he noticed Dirk's truck was still in front of the building. He'd talk with him later, when he felt a little calmer. But right now he'd go see Mom. After all, he thought, deep down he'd always known he was her favorite.

Dirk

Feeling as if he'd been plunged into the twilight zone, Dirk limply shook Ben's hand and went straight to the men's room and locked the door. His knees felt so shaky and his insides so unsettled that he feared he might lose his breakfast.

He ran cold water and splashed off his face. His reflection in the mirror appeared ashen, his skin pasty next to his dark hair and eyes. Leaning against the sink, he steadied himself as he tried to absorb the news.

And here he'd thought he was coming in to talk about their men's league! Golf–it all seemed so trivial now. Shoot, he could probably buy the whole course if he wanted to. He put down the lid and sat on the toilet, head in his hands, to see if he could plan his next move.

In the world that was shifting right under his feet, one thing was sure: He wouldn't have to worry about his or Nora's job security. If he invested wisely, he could make the money go a long way toward covering education expenses for Carter and Logan.

He thought of Alan, who'd meant so much to their family,

who'd made his mom happy for so many years. When Dirk's own self-esteem had been shattered by his dad's repeated taunts of "Runt," Alan had searched for the best in him. He'd even paid for Dirk's accounting classes in Danville and given him a job when he'd finished. And it had been Alan who co-signed for the mortgage on the little fifty-five-year-old prefab that Dirk and Nora had bought several years ago.

What would his life have been like without Alan, he wondered. He sure was starting to find out. There was a big empty space where Alan should have been, both at work and in his mom's life. But now there was all this money. He felt his stomach rumble again.

His sister, Darcy, who helped run The Boulder, would slap him on the back and tell him he deserved every penny. Maybe he could give some to her and Jeb. With the three girls they'd raised, they'd never had an extra cent. But once the word got out, he'd have to watch out for parasites. People around town would crawl out of the woodwork, pretending to be his friend. He wondered how Barley Fiske, his street-smart crony from high school, would take to the news.

After wiping his face with a rough paper towel, he made his way through the lobby. He tried to appear confident as he waved to Ben, who was attacking a pile of papers on his desk.

Inside the cab of his Ford F-150, Dirk took a deep breath. He needed to get back to work. Pete Nolan would be speculating about why he was taking so long.

Putting the key in the ignition, he imagined what Nora would think. She'd be elated, but sensible. He was sure of that much. The oldest of nine from the thrifty Bakers Corners

Sullivan family, she had rattled off information about her brothers and sisters when he'd taken her to The Boulder after they'd met at a dance his senior year.

"We're all called by our middle names," she'd explained as she scraped every trace of her toffee crunch from her small dish. "What's yours?"

"My what?" He'd gotten lost after she'd told him about a few of her siblings.

"Your name, goofball," she'd giggled.

"Well, Dirk–"

"No, your <u>middle</u> name." She'd given him a look that had made him want to take her in his arms right there in the restaurant. "I might want to use it sometime."

"Thomas. But nobody ever uses–"

"Thomas," she'd repeated slowly as if it were as delicious as her first bite of the ice cream she'd ordered.

No, he thought as he turned the ignition key and revved the engine, he wasn't worried about Nora. She'd definitely have her own ideas about the money, but she wouldn't run through it like a lot of women. He'd give her the news tonight after supper.

But first, he decided as he drove in the opposite direction of Atwater's, he'd tell Mom. She'd steady him, help him get his feet back on the ground. She always had and always would. And that was because, he reminded himself, deep down he'd always known he was her favorite.

Doris

How many times in her life had she gone through these motions, Doris mused as she smoothed out the crust for Ellen Gilchrist's banana cream pie. Oh, Darcy or even her granddaughter, Tiffany, would have done it in a heartbeat, but she'd known Ellen since before high school, and the richest old maid in town always swore she could tell if Doris had handed off the job to someone else in the family.

It was funny how some things never changed. She lifted the dough into the pan and began to crimp the edges. Ellen had gone to Longworth School and had been a friend of Alan's sister, Adele. Those girls felt they were better than anyone else even back then, when Doris had been one of the hard-up "Sweet Briar kids across the tracks" snipping dandelion greens for her family's supper. She and her pals had no use for the Longworth snobs and their superior attitudes.

Now Ellen was the major benefactor of the hospital in town and still wanted nothing but the finest. Doris smiled to herself as she took another soft lump from the bowl and began to prepare a second crust for Ellen and the stodgy old broads of the Rockwell Ladies Club. She knew her pies were indeed the best, and she was glad Ellen knew it, too. Even Violet's crust wasn't quite as flaky as hers.

She stopped rolling for a moment as she puzzled over her the recent odd behavior of her older sister. Last week she'd forgotten to add the sugar to a pumpkin pie she'd baked. She'd never pulled a stunt like that before. Luckily, it had been for Tiffany's birthday, and everyone in the family but Violet thought it was hysterical. She'd merely scowled and left the room.

Pausing, she turned down the country music on her little kitchen radio and listened. Someone had pulled into her driveway. It sounded like—she glanced out the kitchen window—it <u>was</u> Dougie climbing out of his car. Right in the middle of the morning! She opened the back door and welcomed him with a hug.

"Come on in. I've got some fresh coffee." She stood on tiptoe to give him a kiss.

"Hey, Mom." Thinking he looked a little washed out as he sat at his old place at the table, Doris allowed her gaze to rest on this beloved rascal who'd probably brought her more trouble than all her other five kids combined.

She'd always thought he looked just like Bill, only with the blond hair and gray eyes that came from her family. That telltale cowlick at the crown of his head had stood straight up every time he got in trouble as a boy. And although it lay flat and obedient today, she couldn't help but notice an air of edginess about him. She figured he must have some kind of big news to share, when she heard the second engine growl in her driveway.

Glancing outside, she watched as Dirk climbed down

from his truck. What in God's name, she wondered, as a multitude of worst-scene scenarios flashed through her mind. Why were the two of them here at the same time? Her stomach flipped. Atwater's, she thought. That damn Pete Nolan. Had he laid off both her boys?

"Dirk-honey." She didn't have to reach up to plant a kiss on his cheek. After all, he was her baby and the shortest of her four sons. She ran her thumb through the gray streak that had appeared recently to the right of his parted dark hair. Although she thought it gave him a distinguished air, she didn't like seeing any sign of aging in her kids—made her feel too old. She handed him a mug of coffee and motioned for him to join Dougie at the table.

"Playing hooky from work?" she began tentatively. God, she thought, they must have something terrible to tell her. Again, her stomach lurched as she wondered if Denny had been in an accident.

"You guys—everyone in the family's okay, aren't they?" She tried to keep her tone light and casual.

"Oh, yeah, yeah," Dirk swirled his mug thoughtfully. "It's just that something really weird happened to us this morning."

"I don't know about weird, but it's sure never happened before." Dougie's blue eyes met hers, then darted away.

With a quick look that took in both sons, she still found it amazing after all these years how different they were in every way–Dougie, athletic, fair and good looking, always battling his temper and making mischief his entire life. And Dirk, wiry and dark with brown eyes that could size you up faster than you'd like, forever planning every step he took.

44

"It's that nasty Nolan, right?" She slammed her palm on the table. "He can't–"

"Whoa, Mom!" Dirk covered her hand with his. "Don't get all worked up."

She squeezed his fingers, looking at Dougie for reassurance. She supposed if both of them were without jobs, she could help them. After all, Ben Priddy had called her in last week to tell her that Alan had left her more than enough money to take her through the rest of her life.

"Well, then, let's have it." She chugged most of her strong coffee and waited as Dougie hemmed and hawed. Dirk shifted in his chair before he finally cleared his throat.

"It's money." He scratched the left side of his head, as he always did when he was puzzled about something.

"A lot!" Dougie added. "A gift from Alan."

Suddenly lightheaded, Doris leaned over and took a deep breath. Their voices sounded fuzzy and far away when they told her their surprise at Alan's generosity.

"You were like his own boys." Her words seemed to come from somewhere else. "He helped raise you. Gave you jobs." She wiped her moist forehead as they rambled on.

"But so much," Dougie repeated over and over.

"How much?" She finally found the courage to ask.

"Two hundred and fifty thousand dollars," they answered in unison.

"Oh my God!" Suddenly she wanted Alan to be there to hold her. In the background she could hear the oven click to remind her that it was preheated, while Garth Brooks's "Friends in Low Places" filtered softly through the air from her radio. "That's way too much for the two of you to split."

"No, Mom, not for us to share." Dirk's voice was firm and clear. "Apiece!"

She grabbed at the tablecloth as she felt herself slipping from her chair. Later, she learned she'd been out cold before she hit the floor.

Ellen Gilchrist never suspected that Violet had finished baking her banana cream pies that day. Doris was grateful for that but still was "damn mad" that she'd fainted dead away when she heard about the money Alan had left her boys.

"Only time I ever did that was when I was pregnant with Darcy. Right in the middle of the library," she told her sons as she rested on the sofa later that afternoon. "And that was 'cause I had high blood pressure."

"Aw, she's just getting puny in her old age." Violet trudged through the living room, picked up a copy of *People*, and started up the stairs to her room. "I'd better keep an eye on her."

The grins that Dougie and Dirk exchanged did not escape Doris. She knew they loved to hear their aunt spout off about everything from the cost of a stamp to her Medicare supplement.

Doris shooed Dirk away as he tried to straighten the pillows behind her.

"I'm fine now," she objected. "But I <u>did</u> call you to come back over here to tell you some things I didn't get around to saying this morning." She shook her head in self-disgust.

Perched on the edges of the twin overstuffed chairs across

the room, the boys waited expectantly for her message.

"Alan has left you each a ton of money." Stating the obvious, she watched them closely as they nodded.

"I guess we all knew he loved the two of you. We just–" She could feel her nose start to tickle as a lump formed in her throat. She pulled a tissue from her apron pocket and took a moment to compose herself. "We just never realized how much."

Dougie whispered something about how shocked Maria would be, while Dirk remained silent. Doris held up her hand to signal she wasn't finished.

"First, don't be runnin' all over town tellin' people about this. They'll learn fast enough. Oh, go ahead and call your sisters. I'll probably write a note to David." She looked them square in the eye as they nodded and waited expectantly for her next words. No one mentioned Denny.

"But most important of all—and I'll only tell you this once—is put that money away at the bank and think long and hard before you start to spend it." She read their stony acceptance as she paused long enough to let her words sink in. "You know that old saying, 'A fool and his money are soon parted.' Well, don't neither of you be playin' the part of no fool. Understand?"

"No problem." Dougie gave her a peck on her cheek. "I've really gotta run, Mom. Maria should be home from school by now." Doris watched her son hesitate at the door, the way he used to do when he tried to psych himself up for a long day in first grade. My God, she thought, he realizes he's in over his head.

"You know, Mom, I'll be careful," Dirk promised as he

leaned over to give her a hug. "You can count on it."

She sighed, assured that Dirk would put the money to good use. After all, next to David, he was the most cautious of all of her kids.

"I mean it!" She hoped to heaven they heard her as they closed the back door quietly behind them.

That evening, she still was so shaken by the news of Alan's gift that she couldn't concentrate on anything else. As she finished a cup of chicken noodle soup, she felt she needed to talk with someone—and not Violet. Her sister would just bang around and make some sharp remarks to let her know that <u>she</u> wouldn't have minded being included in someone's will.

Thank God for email, she thought as she sat down at the computer on her kitchen desk. Punching in the addresses of her old friends, Kate, Rosie, and Cheryl, she considered her words. As always, she wished that writing came as easy to her as cooking. Maybe it would have been, she rued, if she hadn't dropped out of school to marry Bill before her junior year.

Hi!

That was the easy part. Debating how to say what was on her mind, she finally began pounding the keys.

O my god, you guys won't never guess what happened to-day. Dougie and Dirk came to tell me Alan left them a pile of $$ and I passed out rite on the kitchen floor. Don't think I'm pregnant this time. Ha ha. It's a shitload of money. $250,000 *for each of them!!! Not going to tell anyone else but you guys how much. People talk to much.*

Scares me. Dirk will do OK with his, but you know my Dougie. Told both of them to put it in the bank. Won't sleep much tonite, worrying to much. Need to hear from you.

Best friends forever—Doris

Doug

When he threaded his car into the overstuffed garage, Doug was relieved to see that Maria's bike was gone. She'd never given him any grief over the time he spent with Nick or some of the stunts he'd pulled in the past, but he'd never brought her any news like this, either. He wanted to present it to her gently, ceremoniously, like a bracelet he might have bought down at Walt Hamilton's House of Jewelry.

He checked the refrigerator and was glad to see they still had leftover pizza from last night. He'd like to tell Maria over a big steak with sautéed mushrooms, but this would have to do. Opening a bottle of Miller's Genuine Draft, he wiped the cold sweat from the brown glass onto his jeans, welcomed the cool liquid as it washed down his throat, and paced the living room. When should he tell her? How should he tell her? He'd call his sister, Debbie, in Champaign after supper before she heard the news from someone else. But this was now—and he wanted to do it perfectly.

He considered slapping a sticky note on her plate. He wondered about snipping a bouquet of lilacs and telling her when he presented them to her. He debated about waiting until they were settling down next to each other in bed. Maybe that would be the best way.

"Hey, good lookin'!" Maria let the screen door slam behind her as she strode into the living room and planted a kiss squarely on his lips. Sighing contentedly, he welcomed the softness of her body, still warm from her ride.

"Anything new? You seem a little—I don't know—done in." She tucked a lock of her hair behind her ear and backed away to study him.

"Alan left me two hundred and fifty thousand dollars." He heard the words tumble from his mouth. Damn, he thought, he'd never been able to keep a secret.

Speechless, she lowered herself to the couch. Her startled blue eyes showed disbelief. When she spoke, it was in the tolerant tone she saved for her pupils.

"Don't mess with me, sweetie. I've had a helluva day at school."

He sat beside her, his hand resting lightly on her thigh.

"I've never been more serious in my life. That's what Ben Priddy wanted to tell me."

Searching her eyes, he realized she needed time to reflect.

"I'll zap the pizza," he assured her. She always loved it when he took over in the kitchen.

They ate in silence, the subject of Alan's gift hanging like an unacknowledged fog above them. He almost wished she'd yell, the way Tonya always had after every little thing.

"Pizza's soggy," she observed. "It's always better when you do it in the oven."

He nodded and sipped his beer as she remained deep in

thought. At last she stated the obvious.

"That's a lot of money!"

"I know–"

She held up her hand, a signal that she hadn't finished speaking.

"Did you tell your mom?"

Again, he nodded. "She told me to put it in the bank."

"Always the practical one." She smiled slightly.

"Priddy'll have it in my account by tomorrow. It may already be there," he reassured her.

She picked up their plates and carried them to the sink.

"I–I just don't want it to make any difference—you know, with us." She began to cry softly.

He came up behind her, wrapped his arms around her, and kissed the back of her neck. "It won't, babe. Actually, it'll make everything better. We can take a big trip, buy a brand new house–"

She turned and placed her finger over his lips.

"That's just it, kochany. I like things the way they are now." Her words spilled out. "I don't <u>want</u> a new house. I want to fix up this one."

God, he thought, he felt so helpless.

"We won't do anything different." He tried to reassure her. "I don't want to mess with what we have now."

"What I'm saying," she continued, "is this money's <u>yours</u>. Not your mom's, not mine, not Debbie's, or Dirk's or–"

"He left Dirk the same," he interrupted.

Her eyes grew wide. "Wow!" She swallowed. "That's great. But this is yours—and nobody—not Priddy or Nick or anyone—should tell you what to do with it."

"I probably won't touch it till we're old and gray." He kissed her to confirm his promise.

"One more thing," she said as she slipped away from him. "I'd really like to have that set of dishes I saw at Target. But nothing else."

"No problem." He felt a sense of relief and anticipation wash through him. "It's as good as done."

Dirk

Through the open windows of his cozy white house, Dirk could hear his family arguing.

"I'll do it after supper!" Carter protested. "The other guys're playing down at the park. Right now."

"Homework first!" Nora spat out every syllable. "You know the rules."

"But, Mom–"

"No buts," his wife barked as he opened the door. He knew now was not the time to tell her his news.

"And you–" she turned to him. "Go pick up the lantanas. Mr. Holloway called and said they came in today."

Without a word, he returned to his truck. Shoot, he wondered, was Nora going through the change already? She'd sure been crabby lately, talking about taking another night class in Danville and accepting a committee job with the county Democrats. Why couldn't she be happy with things the way they were?

At the nursery, he paid Clell Holloway and shoved Nora's lantanas into the back of his truck. Still preoccupied with his own affairs, he barely heard Clell tell him he might have to look somewhere else for his seedlings next year.

"Me 'n the missus are sellin' out and goin' to Sebring," Clell explained. "This is too daggone much work."

Stunned, Dirk wished him luck and vaguely wondered where he'd buy all his plants from now on. As he drove through town, he hoped the mood at home would be brighter than when he left.

At supper he felt as if the four of them were playing a game and he was holding the trump card. His news that Clell was selling the nursery aroused only minor interest. Nora shrugged and said they could get their seedlings in Danville next spring, then went on to chide Carter about his bad attitude toward his homework and scold Logan about stuffing his mouth too full. After cleaning their plates and finishing their homework quickly, the boys took off to join the neighborhood ball game while the daylight still held.

He admired the way Nora kept a tight rein on their sons. After growing up in a houseful of boisterous siblings with no rules, she was determined to produce a couple of upstanding young men. He felt lucky that the two of them had agreed on most major issues, like how to raise their kids. Long ago, they'd taken control of their lives by waiting to marry until he'd finished his accounting classes, while she'd kept books at the Freeman brothers' grain elevator. Methodically, they stashed away their earnings for a few years before they started their family.

Nora was the best thing that had ever happened to him, he reflected as he stood beside her drying the dishes she placed in the drainer. Only lately had he ever sensed any unrest in his wife—a strange feeling he'd had over the last year that she yearned for something more.

Maybe it was because her entire family had gradually migrated west. As the only remaining Sullivan in the Rockwell area, she'd decided she was the one who'd have to make a difference. When she'd tried to share her feelings with Dirk after signing up to help with the Democratic campaign the previous fall, he hadn't found the courage to tell her John Kerry didn't stand a chance. And now she'd gotten her Irish up and insisted on lantanas instead of their usual zinnias and nasturtiums—not a good sign. Not a good sign at all.

Half-listening as she rambled on about the changes at work that Cargill had made at the old Freeman elevator, her desire to take a sociology course at Danville, and her excitement about the next political campaign, he broke in at last.

"Well, I've got news, too," he announced, dropping the last of the forks in the silverware drawer.

"Yeah?" She continued attacking the ridge of mashed potatoes that stuck to the side of the pan she was scrubbing.

"I went to see Ben at the bank today."

"Oh, yeah? Got your league under control?" She rinsed out the pot and handed it to him.

"No, it was about money." He kept his eyes on the pan he was wiping.

"Money?" she flared, sparks flying from her green eyes. "We've got no money problems. Our bills are paid–"

He placed his dry hands over her sudsy ones.

"Alan left Doug and me some money. I need to tell you about it." He guided her to one of their wooden kitchen chairs, then pulled up another one and sat beside her. "It's big—something neither of us ever planned on."

As he proceeded to describe his meeting at the bank that morning, he saw the magnitude of Alan's gift begin to register on her face. Pale under her freckles, she first was shocked, skeptical, then overjoyed.

"Do you realize what this means? We can build up the boys' college funds, take a family vacation." She sobered slightly. "Maybe even contribute to a worthy cause."

He rose and took her in his arms, savoring every second. A moment like this only came along once in a lifetime.

"We can do all of that—and more. We'll plan it all out on paper–"

Seizing him, she gave him a lingering kiss that lasted until the back door banged and Logan yelled, "I'm thirsty!"

Their son stopped in his tracks as they jumped apart. "Ooh, yuk!" Hastily, he grabbed a bottle from the fridge and escaped to rejoin his friends.

The next evening as he searched for Ben Priddy in the crowd at Rigoni's, Dirk spotted Doug on a bar stool. Ben had wanted to meet with him there to discuss pairings and handicaps over a cold beer but had warned him he might be late. Deciding he'd chew the fat with his brother while he waited, Dirk tapped him on the shoulder.

Doug whirled around, flashed his patented smile, and gave him a high five.

"Hey, bro! How ya doin'?" He lowered his voice to a whisper as he patted the stool beside him. "You feeling like me—up there on cloud nine but kinda walking on eggshells?"

Signaling for a beer, Dirk nodded and sat down next to him. He straightened the appetizer card in the holder on the counter. "You talk to Darcy?"

"Yep—had breakfast there this morning. Told her when I paid my bill." He grinned. "She whooped so loud that people stared. Said she was real happy for us, said I'd have to start ordering the steak sandwich instead of her cheapest hamburger, now that I could afford it."

Dirk laughed. "That's Darcy, all right." He drew a smiley face in the condensation on the side of his mug. "I called Debbie last night in Champaign. It was kinda late, but I knew she'd be up watching one of her sci-fi shows."

Doug raised an eyebrow.

"She squealed, then told me just like mom to spend it wisely. She should know." He thought of his older sister, who'd started with nothing and now owned three beauty salons and had a longtime relationship with a geology professor at the University of Illinois.

"She did say I oughtta take Nora and the boys on a cruise."

"Whatever floats your boat." Doug took a long swig from his mug. "No pun intended."

"Well, look what the cat drug in."

Swiveling on his barstool to see who was talking, Dirk was surprised to see Denny standing behind them. "Hey, Grouchy. Runt." His sneer was filled with the pleasure of knowing he was yanking their chains.

Dirk swallowed hard and noticed Doug clenching his jaw at the sound of their dad's disgusting nicknames. In his head, Dirk could hear Spud reminding him, "Don't take the bait."

"Hey–a booth opened up. Let's talk over there." Doug was always quick to recover in any social situation.

"I can stay with you till Ben shows up," Dirk agreed reluctantly.

Denny tipped his "Born to Raise Hell" cap at the bartender and directed him to put his mug on Doug's tab. "Never turn down the hospitality of a bro." Along with Denny's malicious grin, Dirk noticed the familiar conniving glint in his brother's eyes.

"You planting mostly corn again this year?" Doug began on a safe topic.

"Got to." Denny licked the foam from his top lip. "That and some soybeans."

Dirk remained silent while his older brothers bantered about crops. He'd always bristled when Denny made fun of the garden Dirk cherished, calling him a "farmer wannabee." When Denny threw out another topic, he choked.

"People's talkin' about the two of you," Denny stated calmly.

"Yeah?" This time it was Doug who was taking the bait, Dirk realized.

"They're sayin' that the two of you's come into some money."

Dirk tried not to register any emotion as Denny's eyes settled on him.

"Can't believe everything you hear," Doug remarked. "People make up all sorts of crap."

"Nobody's told me nuthin'. I ain't got a thing against the two of you, but nobody's said nuthin' to me. Not neither of you. Not Darcy. And sure not Mom." Denny waited while his words settled like dust from a revved-up truck. "If I'm still in this family, I guess I'd like to know."

"You're right." Dirk pulled himself up taller in the booth and looked directly at this brother who'd never succeeded at anything except hurting their mom. "We should've told you, the same way we did Darcy and Debbie. Mom's going to write to David."

"Like it'll make any difference to him." Denny's scoff was bitter. "Sittin' down there in Atlanta with the piles of money he gets from his cushy job. He always did think he was better'n me 'n Dad, always jumpin' in to take Mom's part when we was little."

"Yep. And the same bro who's always sent the money to the hatchery to cover your feed tab so you could keep a flock of chickens." Dirk could hear the edge in his own voice. "The same bro who paid Carter's extra medical bills when he had pneumonia a few years ago."

He knew Denny still felt he had extra clout in the family because he was the oldest, but he wasn't going to let him get away with cheap shots at David. If they'd all turned out like his favorite brother, their mom never would have had a worry in the world.

"Whatever." Denny lowered his eyes and stared into his beer.

As the noise level drowned out Kenny Chesney in the background, an uneasy quiet fell on their booth. Doug squirmed uncomfortably, but Dirk felt a sense of calm.

"So here we are," he stated simply. "What do you want to know about the money?"

"Well," Denny drawled as he tugged at the collar of his

plaid shirt, "I guess like . . . is it true?" He glanced away.

Dirk looked at Doug and nodded in agreement.

"Yep," they responded in unison.

"You're going to hear all kinds of figures," Doug added. He glanced at Dirk again for support. Dirk nodded.

"Alan left us each two hundred and fifty thousand dollars. I guess he thought of us as his own sons, working with him and everything. He took care of Mom too–"

Dirk watched while Denny blanched beneath his farmer's tan and fumbled for his mug. The beer sloshed over the rim as he lifted the glass with an unsteady hand.

"No need explainin'," he sputtered. "No need to say nuthin' more. I was wonderin' if the gossip was true. Turns out it was. Only more so."

From the corner of his eye, Dirk could see Ben Priddy approaching.

"I've gotta run," he told his brothers. "Let's do this again sometime."

"Sure." Denny's voice sounded weak and uncertain. "Damn! That sure is a shitload of soybeans!"

A few days later Dirk paused long enough to let the earth ooze between his fingers as he thinned the rows of carrots. Damp from the all-night drizzle, it still felt "better'n Pla-Doh," as he'd told Spud as a child when his uncle had patiently showed him how to smooth the soil gently over a seed.

"It don't matter how tall or short you are when you're

gardening." Spud had adjusted the straps of his bib overalls. "If you can drop in a seed and take care of the plant as it grows, you're as good as a king."

Dirk had puffed out his chest in pride that day when he'd realized that gardening might be the one activity that could put him on equal footing with his older brothers and sisters. Now he moved on to the next row and plucked four small red radishes from the dirt.

"Hey, look!" he called to Nora. "Our first crop of the year. One apiece for supper."

She squinted into the late afternoon sun and gave him a thumbs up.

"I think these lantanas are going to need a little more space." She surveyed the first corner she had planted, then dropped to her knees to make the holes farther apart. "I've heard they really bush out."

Dirk remained silent. If she'd gone with zinnias and nasturtiums the way they'd planned, she'd know exactly how much room to allow. Dismissing that thought, he checked the size of the lettuce leaves and strolled by Nora as she finished her first corner.

"You're always happier when you're playing in the dirt." She tamped the soil around the three plants. "You oughtta buy Clell Holloway's nursery."

He felt the back of his neck grow warm, grateful that Nora was too preoccupied to see the flush that crept up his face. He didn't want to admit that he'd had that very same thought when Pete Nolan had given him some weak numbers to crunch at work that afternoon.

"Yeah, right," he shouted over his shoulder as he ambled

toward the house. "Want me to pick up a pizza at Barley's? We need something to go with these radishes."

"Sure," she called from the farthest corner. "Get the super large, with one section of veggie for me."

Dirk washed his hands, phoned in the order, and hopped into his truck. The pizza would be almost ready by the time he got to Barley's. Shoot, someday he'd have to tell him about the money. He didn't look forward to that.

Bart Franklin Fiske, Jr., son of the only optometrist in Rockwell, had been dubbed "Barley" since high school, when he'd generously doled out his old man's liquor to the Rockwell High athletes who dropped in to play pool in the Fiskes' basement. Although he had never grown more than the 5'9" he'd reached when he was a freshman, Barley still had that youthful swagger and gleam in his eye. As he turned toward the pizza parlor, Dirk speculated about what choice bit of local gossip might be Barley's main topic of conversation today.

They'd always had a special relationship—he and Barley–although his mom had spotted the guy's lack of integrity right on.

"It's okay to help him with his homework," she'd warned him all through school, "but don't be hangin' around that kid too much. I don't want you pickin' up his ways."

Although Dirk had never told his mom about his friend's "massaging the facts," as Barley always liked to call it, she always seemed to be up on everything anyway. She knew when Barley'd been suspended for cheating on tests or running a betting game from the school cafeteria. Dirk realized he'd never have been one of Barley's buddies if Dr. Fiske hadn't paid him for tutoring his son in math. After Dirk saved Barley's hide on a semester algebra exam their freshman year, Barley'd never failed to stand up for him against the school's worst bullies. If it hadn't been for that early bit of bonding, the two most likely would have coasted through Rockwell High without ever noticing each other.

"Howzit look?" Barley held out the mammoth steaming pizza for Dirk to inspect when he walked through the door.

Glancing at the huge round pie, Dirk noted an ample supply of toppings. Barley had a community-wide reputation for skimping on the amount of extras he placed on his pizzas. He was surprised that Barley himself had come out of the office to serve up the order.

"Great, as usual." As Dirk dug into his wallet, he considered how lucky Barley was that his parents had set him up with the franchise when he'd left college after a two-year string of academic failures and a growing mountain of credit-card bills. He was surprised that Barley had kept the business running so long, but then Dirk never pursued the rumors he heard about the side attractions Barley operated from his back room.

"I hear you've had a spot of good luck, my friend." Barley's pointed features seemed more foxlike than usual as he shifted the unlit cigar he always held in his mouth.

"Like what?" Dirk felt his stomach lurch. Barley couldn't know—

"Like coming into a load of money." Barley's beady eyes covered him in one quick glance. "Denny came in to pick up a pizza and said I ought to ask you about it."

Shoot, he thought, his oldest brother was always stirring

up trouble.

"Yeah, well you know how often I talk to Denny." Dirk scooped his change from the counter and grabbed the warm box. "Thanks, Barley—and don't believe everything you hear."

He wiped the sweat from his brow as he started the truck. The topic of money made him nervous. And that wasn't the only thing. As he drove past the grain elevator, he realized how much his wife's recent behavior was gnawing at him.

He and Nora had always been called the "perfect couple" by everyone who knew them—same height, same goals, same dispositions. But lately—well, since he'd encouraged her to take that government class at the junior college in Danville and work toward a degree—she'd seemed restless, ready to embrace a cause merely for the sake of change. Like ordering lantanas instead of zinnias and nasturtiums. And veggie pizza instead of the three-meat special. He liked things the way they were—except for Pete Nolan's inability to run Atwater's. But no amount of hoping and praying was going to bring Alan back.

"You gotta believe this makes our table look kinda little." Nora grinned as she lifted the lid and set the radishes in the center of the pizza. "To celebrate the bounty of our garden," she chuckled as Carter and Logan each snatched a fourth of the pie.

They quickly reduced Barley's "super large" to a few scraps of crust as Carter talked about his next junior varsity game, and Logan interrupted with information about his upcoming class field trip to the Museum of Science and Industry in Chicago.

"Don't talk with your mouths full," Nora chided several times before they carried their empty plates to the sink and dashed out the back door.

In the sudden quiet, as he bagged up the trash, Dirk asked, "You tell anyone today?"

"Not a soul. Thought it would kill me." Nora wiped the counter.

Looking at each other earnestly, Dirk replied, "We've gotta talk."

Alone at their kitchen table, they shared their shock and joy over Alan's gift. Their first priority, they agreed, was to set aside a few thousand dollars in the boys' meager college funds.

"I've been thinking too–" Dirk felt he needed to unload the thoughts he'd had at work that day.

"Shush." Nora reached across the table for his hand. "Out there in the garden? What I said? I was dead serious."

"About–about Holloway's?" He took a deep breath. "I'm not sure . . ."

Again she quieted him. God, he loved it when her green eyes had that serious, "I'm-on-a-mission" look.

It was as if she'd rehearsed her speech all day, he thought, as she suggested that he talk with Clell Holloway and find out his asking price. If it was in the right ballpark, he could get Ben Priddy's opinion.

"We both know your job's on shaky ground," she reminded him. "Everyone down at the elevator's wondering how Pete Nolan's gonna fill Alan's shoes."

"I wonder what Mom would think." He couldn't help but recall his mother's warning to be careful with his money.

"If it's a good business deal, she'll love it." Nora squeezed his hand. "Remember, she took a big leap herself once— when she left your dad. You were too little to remember."

"But she had Spud and Violet as a safety net," he reminded her.

"And you've got me, Thomas." She reached over and kissed him on the cheek. "You've always got me."

Doug

May

He hadn't meant to fall in love. He and Nick had already savored a perfect day on Lake Michigan with the warmth of the sun erasing the winter pallor on their faces, the smoothness of the water lapping against the boat and, always, Chicago's inviting skyline beckoning like a seductive woman. The only thing missing was Maria, who'd passed on their invitation so she could stay home and finish decorating.

"Helluva wife you've got there," Nick had observed earlier in the day. "She gives you all the space you need. And she even likes Harleys and NASCAR."

Doug had grinned. He knew he was one lucky dude, all right.

After a day of cruising, when a chill began to creep through their windbreakers, Nick signaled he was going back to the harbor. When Doug hopped onto the pier with the ropes in his hand, he spotted her.

She hadn't been there when they'd left. But there she was, a stately Sea Ray spilling out of one of the larger slips and gleaming white against the shadowed red string of Inland Steel buildings. He trained his eyes on the sharp navy-blue stripe accented in gold as he walked over to check her name. Shielding his eyes from the late afternoon sun, he read the black script letters outlined in vivid yellow. "Bonnie Sue" she was, with a sassy sunflower dotting the "i" in her name.

"Damn!" Doug whistled softly.

"I'll say." Nick tied up the front ropes. "Cream of the crop. Hey, I'll go fetch the trailer so we can head for home."

"Not too fast." Curious, he stepped closer to read the white card in the front window. "Look. It's for sale."

"Good time of year to sell. Early in the season." Nick sauntered closer and nodded appreciatively. "Looks like she's got about everything a guy'd want. Except boobs." Chuckling at his own humor, he trudged off toward his mini-van.

Doug wasted no time. This feeling had hit him only once before—the day at kindergarten when he'd met Maria. He strode to the office and fired one question to the guy behind the counter.

"How much you want for that Sea Ray out there?" He heard the words coming like little puffs from his own mouth.

"Oh, that beauty? Hell, we're not sellin' her. Wish we was though." Plump and deliberate, the manager chewed each word as he motioned toward the door to the adjoining yacht club. "Owner's in there for a few minutes." When he caught Doug's skeptical expression, he assured him, "Go ahead. Ring the buzzer. They'll let you in."

He felt his confidence begin to slough off when he approached the entrance to the private quarters. Glancing outside, he saw Nick tinkering with his trailer. As he paused with his finger over the button, a silver-haired man in a monogrammed L.L. Bean jacket stepped from the building and held the door open. Doug decided to take a chance.

"That your Sea Ray out there?"

"Not for long."

As the man removed his cap and raked his fingers through his well-cut wavy hair, Doug felt he should know this guy. He'd seen this face before, but bigger, bolder. Those keen blue eyes were now softened.

"I've just put it up for sale. My—my wife died six weeks ago." Doug knew he'd heard that voice. Deep, resonant, it was as familiar to him as Nick's. The man shrugged in the direction of the boat. "That was my wife's name, 'Bonnie Sue.' It won't be the same now."

"I'm sorry. Really sorry for you." As Doug studied the man, he noticed this poor guy wore the same bewildered expression as his mom had since Alan's death. "Good luck to you." He stuck out his hand. "Doug Lochschmidt."

"Cam Watson," the man replied. His eyes sharpened as they studied Doug. "Would you like to see her—the 'Bonnie Sue?' She's been my pride and joy for the last few years."

Doug felt as if a mammoth wave had washed up from the lake and smacked him right across the face. Cam Watson, of course! This was Campbell Watson, former CBS anchor who had delivered the news into their living room for years. Mom had lived and died by his sign-off words, "And that's the news from around Chicagoland and all the world beyond."

"Uh, yeah. Yeah, that'd be cool." He fought off his desire to gape. "Uh, uh, lemme help my buddy load up his boat and we'll be right back."

Like ten-year-olds touring a major-league ballpark, he and Nick boarded the "Bonnie Sue" and tried not to show their awe as Campbell Watson guided them through the forty-two-foot pleasure boat.

"Sleeps six—two in the queen room, two in the twins and two on the seats. Could squeeze in a couple more if you wanted to."

Doug felt as if he were attending a professional presentation as he listened to Campbell Watson's rich tones describe his beloved boat. Running his hand over the smooth white seats with navy piping, he drank in the beauty of the wood-trimmed dashboard.

"How many hours you got on this?" Nick wondered. He nodded as Watson told him three hundred fifty–about right for a 1998 model that had been enjoyed every summer.

"How much?" Doug questioned. When Watson turned and raised an eyebrow in the manner of one used to making deals, Doug repeated. "How much do you want for it?"

"I'm asking one sixty-nine."

Doug left the two at the stern and wandered through the cabin. He could picture himself standing behind Maria as she steered along the Lake Michigan shoreline. He saw their friends and family laughing together every weekend. A vision of Darcy and her husband popped before him when he imagined his hard-working sister giggling as she bounced across the waves.

He could make it all happen. All he had to do was dicker with Campbell Watson on the price, and he'd be a hero to everyone he knew. Even Nick. Especially Nick. Hell, he thought, the money in his account was beginning to make him nervous anyway.

"I'll give you one sixty-four." Doug hadn't felt this sure of himself since the day he'd married Maria.

"Dude!" Nick sputtered.

"Are you sure you can– Maybe you'd better check with your banker first." Even the polished Campbell Watson seemed unsettled by his abrupt offer.

"Nope," Doug assured him. "I could write you a personal check this afternoon if you like." He reached for the checkbook inside the lining of his windbreaker.

"I was going to stand firm at one sixty-nine." Now Campbell Watson was rubbing the famous cleft in his chin and talking to himself as his blue eyes evaluated Doug. "But I think my wife would like you, kid. She'd be happy for you to have the boat." He patted the back of the captain's seat. "We've had some of the best times of our lives on the 'Bonnie Sue.'"

Doug felt a tug at his sleeve.

"Dude, you can't do this. I mean not so fast!" Beads of sweat stood out on the face of the usually unflappable Nick. "You've gotta talk this over with Maria. Even Priddy."

"No problem." Doug felt calm and relaxed as he explained that his wife would understand and that the only conversation he'd have with Priddy would be to tell him to wire the money to Watson's account. He couldn't wait to see the expression on ol' Priddy's face when he realized Doug had been dealing with the Campbell Watson.

At Watson's suggestion, they sought out the manager at the counter and asked him for a sheet of paper. In neat block letters, the newsman drafted a sales agreement that both signed. Doug shook hands and promised to finalize the transfer of funds first thing Monday morning.

The manager tried to steady his trembling hands as he made a copy for each of them. "Looks like you got more'n a snack in the clubhouse." Peering at Cam Watson, he measured his words carefully. "Got yourself a buyer is what you did."

Doug grinned and assured Watson they'd be in touch on Monday. As he and Nick headed for the mini-van, he felt this was the best thing he'd done since marrying Maria.

"Toss me the keys and I'll drive," he said to Nick. "You look kinda shaky."

Dirk

"Still needin' sumpin' special?" Clell Holloway set down his sprayer and ambled among the rows of herbs in the greenhouse. "Thought you prob'ly had everything for this season."

Dirk swallowed hard and tried to appear nonchalant.

"My wife thought she might like some rosemary and basil," he lied.

"Herbs is gettin' real popular these days." Clell pinched off a couple of dry leaves. "Thought you was the guy from the Danville <u>Commercial-News</u> when I heard you drive up."

Dirk knew Clell was begging to be asked, so he scratched his head and invented a question.

"Are they doing a story on you?"

"Nope." Clell snugged up a strap on his overalls. "I'm puttin' an ad in Sunday's paper." He nodded toward the back of the greenhouse. "You know. For all this."

Picking up a small container of thyme, Dirk sniffed its pungent leaves.

"What's 'all this' include?" He tried to make his question

sound casual.

Clell shrugged. "All the stock you see here plus the greenhouses and equipment. And the land they're on, of course. Includin' that little brick outbuilding plus everything that's in there."

"Not your house?" Dirk thought Clell would want to sell the whole thing as a package.

"Naw." Clell surveyed his two-story home, a building that Dirk knew a real estate agent might describe as a "carpenter's dream."

Clell went on to explain that a young couple with four kids had asked to buy it on a land contract.

"My greenhouses are prob'ly in better shape than the house," he added, "but those folks didn't want nothin' to do with 'em."

Dirk placed his two pots of rosemary and basil on the counter. "How much?"

"Eight dollars and sixteen cents," Clell answered.

"Not the plants." Dirk could feel his face reddening. "I meant for the business."

Clell's hand hovered over the cash register as he hesitated in the middle of the transaction.

"One hundred and eighty-nine thousand dollars. Firm." He squinted at Dirk. "Know anybody who'd be interested?"

"I might." Dirk pocketed his change. "I'll see," he added as he headed for the door.

"Hey!" Clell called abruptly. "Ya forgot somethin'."

Dirk turned and saw the old man patting the counter.

"Your plants."

"Oh. Thanks." Dirk blushed at his forgetfulness. "Guess

I've got my mind on too many things."

"Guess so," Clell agreed.

The responsibility of his new fortune haunted Dirk's dreams throughout the next week. Each night he broke into a sweat when a leering Barley offered to sell him the pizza business. He battled his blankets when Denny snarled repeatedly, "What're you goin' to do with all that cash?" Around four every morning he awakened with such a start that he couldn't get back to sleep.

Trying to grasp the fragment of a plan—any plan–from his dreams, he sought advice from each person whose opinion he valued.

Nora told him this was the chance he'd been waiting for to be his own boss. He agreed.

His mom warned him to look over Clell's figures from the past "real good" to make sure he wasn't buying "no pig in no poke." He agreed.

And when Ben Priddy swiveled in his banker's chair, stared out the window, and advised, "Get his tax figures, and let's see. Hell, Dirk, you wouldn't even need a loan," he agreed to that too.

His stomach lurched when he saw Clell's ad in the paper that Sunday. What if somebody beat him to it? Nora and his mom had given him their blessings, but Ben seemed to need several days to go over Clell's past returns. Dirk was puzzled. He worked with figures and felt it shouldn't take a banker that long. Finally, after he'd studied the ad for the

fifth time, he was so antsy that he called Ben with a manu-
factured question about their golf league that week.

"Had a chance to look over those figures from Clell?" he
asked during a lull.

"Oh, yeah. I was planning to let you know tomorrow at
work." Ben's tone was casual, as if he might be giving him
information about their tee time. "Looks pretty good. The
year-to-year consistency's there. That's what I wanted to
see."

The next morning, after another sleepless night created
a surge in his adrenalin, he drove to Clell's during his lunch
break. In the damp, musty air of the greenhouse, the two
debated the different qualities of thyme before Dirk blurted,
"I'll give you one hundred seventy for it."

"Make it one seventy-five and you've got yourself a deal
you'll never regret." Clell swallowed hard and looked away.
"Me 'n the missus have made a good livin' off this place."

They sealed it with a handshake. As Dirk felt Clell's
weathered grip in his own, he knew he'd made the right decision. This—all of it, full of growing things that promised
to give his life a sweet new flavor—would be his.

When Nora joined him at home after work, she slapped
him a high-five, then planted a kiss on his lips. "You gotta
believe this is something we can all work on. As a family.
Together."

Carter and Logan merely wolfed down their supper and
asked if they'd get paid for some of their tasks before they
left to join the neighborhood ball game.

"You didn't waste any time," Ben kidded him when Dirk stopped in at the bank to share his news. "I'll get our attorney to draw up some papers, and you and Clell can sign them right here in my office. One more thing though—don't think about all this when you're putting for a birdie, okay?"

The reaction from his mom was the one he valued most. Wrapped in her motherly bear hug, he hung on every word.

"I'm so proud of you, Dirk-honey. You've found a good place to put Alan's money and you've checked out all the financial angles."

He felt himself glowing in her praise as she continued.

"I've done a bit of riskin' in my lifetime, you well know. Leavin' your dad when I had to. Startin' up The Boulder with Violet. Hangin' on to Alan for—well, for everything that mattered." She brushed her cheek with her sleeve. "But I've never regretted none of it. And I know you'll feel the same."

"Thanks, Mom." He embraced her once more and promised he'd see her in a day or so.

"Dougie's comin' over in a little bit," she added. "Didn't say what he wants. Maybe he'll learn somethin' from you, get himself set up in a good business."

"Hope so, Mom." He grinned and closed the screen door softly behind him. As he walked across her driveway, he realized that all he had to do now was give Pete Nolan his notice. That'd be a moment to savor, for sure. He and Clell would sign the papers, then the nursery would be his. He might even be running the place before the Fourth of July.

A momentary shadow fell across his sunny future as he wondered if he and Nora would be able to make it to his mom's annual mandatory picnic. They might need to work on the holiday. Shoot, he thought, he'd cross that bridge when he came to it. One day at a time. The business was his to run.

He felt a foot taller as he climbed into his truck.

Doris

May

Hi!

You all won't never believe this. But I just gotta tell someone before I blow up and have to go to the ER to get my blood pressure taken care of.

Doris pondered her next words as she sat hunched over her computer. Hell's bells, she thought, it would have been easier just to call all of 'em. But Cheryl most likely wouldn't be at home, and Rosie'd be mad if she got interrupted during "Jeopardy." Kate seemed to have to help Marty more and more these days, and Doris didn't want to bother her. She sighed, plunged in, and let her feelings do the talking.

You know Alan left Dougie and Dirk a bundle when he died. Way to much. Here's what happened. Dirk, bless his heart, spent his in a hurry but had some common sense. He bought Clell Holloway's greenhouses so him and his wife and kids could run it as a family business. His pal at the bank checked all the figures and said it's OK. I'm proud of him for using his smarts as far as this money is concerned.

But that stupid Dougie! There's not enough cuss keys on this dam computer to say how I feel about him rite now. *$#+ He just came and told me he went and blew his wad on a boat. A *%# boat that he don't know nothing about. SHIT!!!!! At least I can spell that.

He went to Lake Michigan with Nick Rigoni and saw a boat he took a shine to. Just like that he spent most of what Alan left him. On a boat. On a $^# toy!!!!!It don't matter one bit that it belonged to Camull Watson, the TV guy.

Hell, Tonya or Renee couldn't of spent that money any faster. I could ring his neck. Could have set himself up with a nice business like Dirk and he wasted it. Wasted it all.

I'm to *^$@ mad to cry so I'll just sit here and slam this out with as many cuss keys as I can find on this dam thing. Like we used used to say way back when ....FRIED FRITTERS!

Best friends forever—Doris

2006

Dirk

May

"Can you believe this is ours?" Nora snugged herself under his arm and surveyed the rainbow of color in their greenhouse. Her amazement triggered a feeling of pride in his chest.

"I never dreamed something like this could happen." Savoring their contentment of the moment, Dirk also made a mental note to give the impatiens an extra drink the next day. "This is even better than last year," he told her. "'Cause it's <u>ours</u>. Not Clell's leftovers."

He checked his watch, surprised to see it was almost eight o'clock. They'd worked right through supper, making the most of every minute the recent switch to daylight saving time had allowed.

"Dad! I'm starved!" Logan called from the north shed, where he'd been organizing extra trays and containers. "Can we pick up a pizza?"

"Sounds good to me." Nora wiggled from under Dirk's arm. "We'll swing by the ball park and see if Carter's done with practice first. I'm too pooped to cook anyway."

Before they closed the door, she stopped to take one last look at the greenhouse.

"I'd sure hate to pick a favorite," she said softly. "I love the way the pink and yellow snapdragons look next to each other. And, of course," she poked him in fun, "you know I'm still partial to the lantanas."

"No comment." He smiled, knowing he'd never live down his reluctance last year to plant different flowers in the corner of their vegetable garden. Her choice had exploded into mounds of variegated color, proving she'd been right. Good thing, too, he thought, 'cause they'd been too busy at the greenhouse to devote much effort to their own yard. Sometimes he worried he'd become a slave driver, prodding Nora and the boys to nurture every seedling that promised a potential profit.

One sultry evening last July he'd felt his mom's eyes drilling holes in his back after he'd spoken gruffly.

"Don't you dare get like your dad," she'd warned him after he'd insisted that Nora and the boys continue to deadhead their annuals so they'd still look good to a buyer. Wilted from the heat, the three had dutifully plodded down row after row to finish before dark.

"That damn Bill worked me harder in the fields than he did our old tractor!" His mom had grumbled, adding, "Prob'ly knew he could get more on a trade-in for the tractor than he could for a worn-out housewife with six kids!"

Now, as he bundled the cash and checks for the deposit the next day and locked them in the vault, he admitted to himself it was hard to heed his mom's advice. Too much going on that he couldn't control. That was the problem. Carter had signed up for a summer baseball league and been invited to try out for a travel team. That'd put a dent in the budget.

Logan had done so well with his eighth-grade science project that he'd won a scholarship for a week of camp at the U of I. Dirk was downright proud of both boys, but they'd be giving up time that could've been spent in the greenhouse. Shoot, he thought, maybe Mom was right about me. Maybe I'm more like my dad than I'd like to think.

Not really. Checking the doors on the two sheds to make sure they were locked, he recalled he'd kept Tuesday nights open. After all, Ben had declared he'd never approve another loan for the greenhouse if Dirk didn't stay on as his partner.

He waved to Nora as she and Logan took off in her Corolla to pick up Carter. Lost in thought, he almost forgot to call Barley with the pizza order. If the rest of their season went as well as this May, he might never <u>need</u> to ask Ben for another loan. Nora's hunch had paid off when she'd suggested some of the locals might like variety, so they'd dumped Clell Holloway's traditional menu of petunias, geraniums, and marigolds and doubled their wholesale order for verbenas. They'd bought four-inch cubes of lobelias and dahlias that had been snapped up faster than free hotdogs at one of Carter's games. Debbie'd taken a ton of stuff back home with her, telling him his little greenhouse had a better selection of plants than she could find anywhere in Champaign.

As he backed his truck out of the lot, he paused once more to look at the new sign Darcy and Jeb had made for the greenhouse.

"Redbud Hill." The fuchsia letters danced happily across the cream-colored wooden sign. He liked the name they'd picked last summer when his mom had visited the greenhouse for the first time.

She'd taken one look around the place and nodded in approval at his investment.

"You've got yourself a nice piece of property," she'd told him. "All these pretty flowers inside and that bunch of redbud trees up there on the hill. A whole lot better than your brother." She'd tossed her head in disgust.

He'd loved her stamp of approval on his business but had glanced away when she'd mentioned Doug. She never missed an opportunity to take a dig at his big brother for parting so foolishly with his inheritance.

Sometimes, he thought as he headed toward Barley's, he almost felt sorry for Doug. During the winter his brother had groaned, "I should have just called it 'That Damn Boat.' That way, Mom would've at least liked the name!" Doug had sighed and asked when Dirk and his family could join him for a weekend on the water.

"Not this summer," he'd answered. "Too much work to do. Clell left a lot of stuff that needs fixing up. Maybe next year."

He parked the truck outside Barley's.

"Hey, my friend!" Barley greeted him. "Be ready in a flash."

Dirk nodded, inhaling the welcoming aroma of pizza that meant his day was winding down. "I put on extra toppings." Barley puffed out his chest.

Dirk knew the guy meant he'd filled the order the way

he should.

"You being in business sure has been good for me." Barley secured the extra large pie into its box and headed for the cash register. "This is the third time you've been in this week. You must be doin' okay." He squinted at Dirk as he counted out his change.

"If you ever want in on some action, I got some games goin' in the back room. Lots of fun. And lots of money changin' hands sometimes, if you know what I mean."

"Yeah, Barley, I know what you mean. But not tonight. Gotta get this home."

With a practiced hand, he opened the passenger door of his truck and set the box on the front seat. Suddenly, he couldn't get home fast enough. His belly rumbled. And he needed to talk to Nora. If she'd just take those master gardening classes in Danville in the fall, they could offer seminars at the greenhouse next summer.

It was great that his family pitched in the way they did, he realized as he turned down his street. Made for good times together. And for good business. Even better than he'd planned.

Doug

"Next time I hope Kevin Harvick wins," Cherisse whined from the back seat of Doug's Grand Prix. "I hate stupid Jeff Gordon!"

"Gordon's a great driver. And Harvick came in fourth." Maria turned and spoke calmly to their passenger, who'd just finished second grade.

"Fourth place don't mean nothing though. Gordon's stupid anyway."

After he merged onto I-57 and headed south toward Rockwell, Doug rolled his eyes at Maria, signaling to his wife that his granddaughter already knew more about NASCAR than anyone in the family and would just have to wallow in her disappointment.

"Doesn't mean anything." Maria corrected her gently.

"I know." Cherisse sighed. "It was fun though. Thanks, Gramps."

"Wanna go back to Joliet again sometime?" He was glad to hear her change in attitude. "It's a pretty good way to celebrate your eighth birthday."

"Sure do," she answered brightly. "And maybe next year

Harvick'll win!"

He chuckled.

"Just a little competitive," he muttered.

"Like someone else I know." Maria grinned, resting her hand on his thigh.

God, he loved it when she touched him like that. As he tried to focus on the heavy traffic, he couldn't help but realize how lucky he was. They'd celebrated their second anniversary a month ago and still felt like two kids who'd just exchanged 1978 class rings. In the last year, she'd gotten the new set of dishes she'd wanted at Target and encouraged him to enjoy every possible minute on his boat. They could have fixed up the house or taken an exotic cruise, but Maria had suggested he keep the rest of Alan's money in a savings account for operating expenses for the big toy that now awaited them at the marina in East Chicago.

He sure was glad she'd mentioned overhead, he reflected as he sped past the Kankakee exits. He'd kind of freaked out when he got last summer's bill for boat storage and, right on top of it, another one for close to eighteen hundred dollars for this season. He'd decided to scale back his NASCAR ticket order to only the races at Joliet and Brooklyn this year, reminding Maria their weekends were too full. But that was only half the truth. The other half was that he didn't want his bank account running on empty too soon.

Maria sure had been one helluva good sport about the boat so far. She was the one who'd suggested the name that he'd had painted in gold after they'd used it several times as the "Bonnie Sue" last summer.

"You should call it 'Windfall,'" she'd shouted to him as

they sliced through the waves one Sunday early in September.

"Huh?" he'd called back, not quite getting it at first and cutting his speed so he could hear her better.

"Yeah, you know. That's what Alan's money was for both you and Dirk—an unexpected gift." She'd brushed her hair back from her face. "Look at how much fun we're having that we never, ever expected."

"Windfall." He'd turned it over several times. The more he repeated it, the more perfect it sounded. "Damn!" He'd grinned at Maria. "I think you've just named our boat!"

Now he glanced at his wife, dozing after the long, hot day at the race, and softened the volume on Trace Adkins' "A Girl from Texas." Cherisse purred contentedly from the back seat. He sure did love that little girl, but it made him madder than hell when her mom used her as leverage to try to wring more money out of him!

He thought of the time several months ago when Renee had demanded he buy her a new house with his inheritance. Then, when she realized he'd already splurged his funds on the boat, she'd pitched a fit and made him feel guilty for not giving her at least twenty-five thousand dollars to pay off her credit cards.

When that hadn't worked, Renee lied to Cherisse, telling her that Doug and Maria didn't want to see her anymore. Several days later, Maria had asked Cherisse why she seemed so sad at school, and his granddaughter had spilled the beans. Boy, everything had hit the fan after that!

He and his mother had settled the whole thing with a nasty air-clearing in Renee's apartment. Mom had unloaded some of her choice vocabulary, like she was Judge Judy or somebody. Renee had stared them down with hateful looks but finally agreed to let Cherisse spend time with Maria and him again. Renee sure was Tonya's daughter!

Now, pumped from watching his favorite drivers with his two favorite girls, he bumped up his own speed another five miles per hour. Next weekend his granddaughter had opted to stay at her best friend's house, having declared a day on the boat as "a little bit boring." He and Maria were ready to party with Nick and his current squeeze, Amy Cox, and their old high-school basketball teammate, Scott Hellyer and his wife, what's-her-name. A couple of weeks later, Darcy and Jeb were going to join them for some time on the lake.

Damn, he realized as he approached his exit. He really was one lucky dude!

The following Saturday, as Maria offered drinks to their passengers, Doug felt the same satisfying thrill he had each time he turned the key in the ignition—the surge of power as they reached the "big water" when they emerged from the bay, the food that tasted way better than anything on land, the satisfying feeling of knowing he was making it all possible.

Although Maria had the routine down pat—carryout pizzas the first evening, fixings for breakfast the next morning, and sandwich stuff and snacks before they docked—there sure was a different atmosphere every time they launched.

Except for the fact that Nick and Amy had called to cancel at the last minute because he had to tend bar, today was picture-perfect with temps in the low 80s and only an occasional ripple on the lake. Doug whistled to himself as they churned toward the Chicago skyline, while Scott's wife, Kammi-Sue, held her nose each time wisps of smoke from the Gary mills filtered toward them. She'd taken the seat across from Doug up front, in case she felt queasy from the motion of the boat.

He tried to distract her by pointing ahead to the cluster of skyscrapers carved crisply against the cloudless blue backdrop. He chuckled. It'd worked. Kammi-Sue forgot the industrial odors and asked if they'd be able to see the Magnificent Mile from the lake.

He sure hoped he wouldn't be stuck with her beside him the whole weekend. Although she still had the cute features that had won over his buddy back when they were freshmen at Eastern Illinois, she'd porked out over the years. Somehow, her round face now had a suspicious edge to it, as if she might be expecting bad news any minute. And that nasal voice was enough to shatter a beer mug.

Not like they were gonna indulge in a kegger this weekend, he reminded himself grimly as they slowed to watch the Ferris wheel at Navy Pier. Kammi-Sue had phoned Maria earlier in the week to place their order, so to speak— no beer ("we're Christians, you know"), no mayo on anything ("we don't want to get food poisoning"), and no white bread ("we're eating only one-hundred-percent whole grain, preferably stoneground"). Maria had listened patiently, bought all the required groceries, and then tossed in a box of Twinkies just for spite.

Doug couldn't wait for Scott to spot those little sponge cakes that had been his favorite snack since high school.

Kammi-Sue might be insisting on a heart-healthy diet at home, but one glance at the tire around Scott's middle made Doug realize his old buddy must be cheating on his wife's nutritional plan.

That evening when they dropped anchor in a shallow spot off Chicago's north shore, he lost track of the number of slices of pizza Scott shoved into his mouth while bombarding them with success stories of his sales career with the printing company his dad had founded.

"We're all so proud of Scottie," Kammi-Sue twanged. "He's built us this big beautiful house that you must come see. And he's taken over as the head lay person at our church. There's not a committee or a Bible study that he's not a part of."

"Yep. Somebody's gotta do it." As Scott reached for the diet soda Maria was handing him, he let his fingers linger on her wrist a few seconds longer than necessary.

"So how many years have you two been married?" Maria fixed her schoolteacher gaze on him until he lowered his hand and stared at the floor. "You sure do seem happy together."

Doug almost spilled the beer Maria had brought him and turned away so Scott couldn't see him laugh. When he looked back at his old friend, however, he noticed how thin his fading red hair had become and how those sagging jowls jiggled when he spoke. Right then, Doug realized that—Bible studies or no Bible studies—old Scott must be cheating on more than his diet. It was pretty obvious he'd practiced that move he'd just made on Maria on lots of girls in his sales territory.

Doug smiled as he unwrapped a Twinkie. Maria sure

knew how to settle this sorry old wolf without turning off any of her hostess charm. As he raised the anchor, he couldn't wait to fire up the speed and give their guests a bouncy ride they'd never forget.

If their weekend trip with Scott and Kammi-Sue had been a test of their patience, the cruise two weeks later offered nothing but pure joy. Although the city's skyline appeared fuzzy through a layer of fog, and the breeze threatened to carry their paper plates into the lake, Doug was proud of the way the "Windfall" handled the waves. At least nobody was complaining like that crybaby Kammi-Sue.

Of course, it took a lot to ruffle the feathers of his sister Darcy. He glanced gratefully at her as she passed around the sub sandwiches and platter of spinach dip and chips she'd brought along.

"You're not makin' all the food, for lord's sake," Darcy had scolded Maria on Thursday. "That's one of the things I'm good at, so you just relax and have fun for a change. Me 'n the girls'll whip up something for Sunday, too."

That was <u>so</u> Darcy, he thought as he met a big wave head-on and was glad to feel the "Windfall" barely bobble in the water. He couldn't remember when she was born, 'cause he'd just been two-and-a-half back then, and he couldn't count the number of times he'd heard his mom say that Darcy had been her biggest baby and that she wasn't supposed to have any more—until Dirk showed up fifteen months later.

He marveled at how much Darcy looked like their mother,

only a bigger version, with her light hair and gray eyes. She sure got Mom's work ethic, too, he realized. There she was, with her first and third daughters, Tiffany and Mallory, handing out food like they did at The Boulder. Lindsay, the middle daughter and the spitting image of Aunt Violet, was studying art in Columbus, Ohio, or she'd have joined them. Yep, he thought as he sipped his beer, Darcy and Jeb Coburn, the former star lineman on their football team and now manager of the Rockwell Street Department, had built a solid life for themselves.

"Hey, Jeb—wanna take the wheel for awhile?"

Jeb's face lit up like a kid at Christmas as he lowered his muscular frame into the captain's seat.

"Just hold 'er steady," Doug advised.

"Aye, aye, sir." Jeb gave a smart salute and added, "Later, maybe I can see the engine."

That evening, when the pink and gold rays broke through the clouds for a spectacular sunset, Doug winked at Maria, who responded with a loving invitational smile. He wondered if evenings like these were what he'd been thinking about subconsciously when he'd bought the boat. Family and good times. What could be better?

He promised himself he'd get his sister, Debbie, out here, along with her geology professor significant other who was—in spite of his smarts—a pretty decent guy. He knew Debbie adored Dirk and had driven to Rockwell to see his greenhouse, but she'd always made a place for Doug. Debbie'd rescued him more than once when he'd been in scrapes in high school, even persuading the principal not to put him on probation so their mom wouldn't have to go to bat for him another time. All he'd done was spread Saran wrap on a few of the toilet seats in the girls' restroom and laughed when they'd screamed at the mess! He guessed he owed her several boat rides.

"Hey, big bro," Darcy called over the strains of Carrie Underwood, "sometime it'd sure be cool if we could get all six of us kids out here. Together. And with Mom," she added.

"Wow! That's a great idea!" Maria sat up straight and shot Doug her "let's-do-it" expression. "Maybe next summer, when David's home from Atlanta."

"Sounds like a party to me." Doug could picture it all. Just like this, only better. In the back of his mind, he wondered if Maria would go so far as to invite Denny. She'd mentioned several times that she couldn't tolerate the way his brother treated their mom. We'll see, he thought.

And Mom? She'd go dancing down Vermilion Street in Danville before she'd ever ride in this boat. She was still mad at him for blowing his money and wasn't about to change.

A week later he knew he'd crossed the line when he'd bitched about Pete Nolan's surly attitude once too often. That was all it took for Maria to get it into that pretty little head of hers that he should invite Pete and his creepy family to join them for a day trip.

At first he'd winced and pretended not to hear, sauntering out the kitchen door to the back yard.

"Come back here and listen to me," Maria called in her steady-but-firm classroom voice. She'd then explained that

97

having a little fun together might smooth things over at work.

"You know Pete's a big talker, but I bet he's scared since he's been trying to run the business. He just takes it all out on you." She'd kissed his cheek lightly. "C'mon, kochany. For you. For both of us."

Of course she'd looked so damn cute that he'd agreed. But now here he was–wasting a beautiful Sunday with Pete and his prudish wife, Nyla, along with their two thin-lipped twenty-something daughters, Alicia and Letitia. Thank God it was only a day trip!

As they idled along the north suburban shore, Pete bragged that the Tigers were going to finish ahead of the White Sox and speculated that Atwater's needed to snag some contracts to build a few homes like "these million-dollar babies."

"That'd get us back on track." His boss folded his arms, set his square jaw, and squinted into the sun. His sparse gray crew cut gave him the look of an aging army sergeant. "You need to go after some of that Danville money."

Kicking up the speed so he couldn't hear the babble about the Detroit team that he hated, Doug tried to stay calm and focus on Pete's business ramblings. Like there was all that much money in Danville anymore, he thought. Glancing over his shoulder, he saw Maria politely doling out iced tea and cookies to Nyla and her daughters.

As he wiped some spray from his face, he speculated about those two girls. Although Pete always called them "Alicia" and "Letitia," he'd heard from a good source down at Rigoni's that "Alli" and "Tish" Nolan were, indeed, "pretty hot babes." Both secretaries at Midwest Manufacturing, they accompanied their bosses to several out-of-town conventions. That's where, his buddy had winked and confided, they'd been the "toast of the town."

You sure couldn't tell by looking. Doug sneaked another peek at Pete's two strange daughters. Both were the picture of propriety as they sat stiffly at the far end of the boat, the mist never stirring a hair on their well-sprayed black pageboys. In fact, for all he knew, they might have been mannequins. Still, he had to admit they shared that subtle, come-hither quality he'd seen in a few girls he and Nick had met once when they were invited to a dance at the Danville Country Club. He'd have to ask Maria what she thought.

He was grateful when the wind shifted, delivering the sharp hint of fall.

"Oh, my!" Nyla exclaimed, clutching her cardigan at her throat. "Maybe we'd better go back to the marina."

Doug obliged, turning the boat smoothly and heading back toward East Chicago. He suppressed a grin when he saw the relief on Maria's face. He sure wouldn't trade places with old Pete for anything.

As they docked and climbed onto the pier, Pete patted the "Windfall."

"Nice little tugboat you got there." He snickered derisively. "Makes me wonder how much you really need a job."

Doug could feel the muscle in his cheek start to twitch as he checked to make sure the boat was tied firmly.

"Never take the bait." Once again, Spud's words helped him keep his cool.

"Well, this has been so much fun." Maria gave Pete her warmest smile. "Atwater's sure is lucky to have both of you."

Doug could find no words. He was only glad he wasn't in Pete's shoes, with a broomstick for a wife and God-knows-what for daughters. His own girls had never been angels, but at least they'd never pretended to be something they weren't. Not even Renee.

Damn, he thought as he tried to ignore Pete's words. Sometimes you try to do something nice for someone and it backfires. Maria sure did owe him. Big time!

Dirk

August

He sucked in the sweet aroma of the soil as he stood alone on a humid evening in the greenhouse. Satisfied with the fruits of his labor for the first full season, he now was bursting with plans for the next year. Oh, there'd been ups and downs all summer. He'd almost popped with pride as Carter and Logan pruned overgrown plants and Nora chatted with the steady stream of well-heeled customers who eagerly offered her their credit cards.

But he'd come close to puking when several flats of leggy petunias and heat-exhausted impatiens hadn't sold by mid-July. Most of them had found homes with his old Sweet Briar schoolmates who wanted to spruce up their spotty yards. Barley'd urged him to take them as a tax write-off, but he'd just been glad there were folks who could enjoy them.

The worst moment had come when they had to dump the rest of the flats behind the south shed and plow them under. Fighting back tears, he believed there was plenty of life in those scraggly plants. Such a waste! Still, Clem had warned them it was all part of the business.

The business. <u>His</u> business! There was so much to do in the months ahead. He'd contracted with Pete Nolan to get a good deal on materials to build a second larger greenhouse in October. That way, he and Nora could start a lot of their own plants and cut down on costs from wholesalers. Ben had looked at his projections and given him the green light.

"You've still got cash from Alan's gift, and a small loan from us would do the trick," he'd told Dirk as they'd putted on the eighteenth hole two weeks ago.

He hadn't confided in Ben or even Nora yet, but he'd also made another commitment—to use part of the old greenhouse for a pond section that would draw folks from Danville for sure. He'd struck a good deal with the sales rep by signing early and would talk with Ben about increasing the amount of the loan. Shoving aside his growing concerns about his sons' dwindling enthusiasm, he knew he could pay them extra to help him unpack all the fountains and pumps. He'd deal later with Carter's announcement that he was going to work at McDonald's "for more money" next summer and would try to motivate Logan to focus on the science of gardening.

He blotted his damp brow and decided to abandon the greenhouse's suffocating heat for his air-conditioned office. Nora'd be here any minute to tell him about the fall courses she'd registered for and when the master gardener classes would be offered.

As he switched on his office light, he glanced at the darkening sky. Purple mountains of clouds were building in the west. Persistent rumbles signaling the predicted storm concealed the sound of Nora's car pulling into the parking lot.

"Hey, Thomas!"

Startled to hear her voice, he whirled at the sound of his pet name. Lately, she'd seemed to use it only when she wanted something or was indicating he might get lucky that night. From the way her eyes met his, he felt encouraged about the rest of the evening. Thank God they had air-conditioning at home, he thought.

He hugged her, then offered her a soda from the fridge.

"Gotta tell you about my classes." She took a long sip and perched on the chair across from him.

"Get what you wanted for next term?" he wondered.

"Better than that! You'll never guess." Her green eyes danced as she took a deep breath. "I got in Blumenthal's government class. And—are you ready for this—he's going to let me sit in on his poly sci class, too."

She paused. He realized this was his cue to show elation, but he only knew Blumenthal by his liberal reputation.

"Wonderful." His limp response sailed right by her.

"And I also got the English class I wanted."

He was afraid he was going to have to tether her to the chair to keep her grounded.

"But—but–that's three classes. I thought you were going for two." More pizza orders for Barley, he calculated quickly. Less family time for us.

"I know. But it's what I feel I need to do." Her eyes were earnest. "I'm not quite ready to sit home and knit on winter nights."

"And the master gardening classes?" His words hung

like puffs of humidity that had formed in the cool comfort of his office.

"Oh, I'll do that another time." She dismissed his question with a wave of her hand. "Blumenthal only teaches government every other year. I can't believe my good luck!"

Whirling around the room, she celebrated as he tried not to sulk. Shoot, all their plans for her to conduct customer workshops were gone. Just like the plants they'd had to dump.

"Hey, Thomas." She studied him as she dropped her soda can in the recycling tub. "You don't look all that excited." The first splots of rain drummed on the tin roof.

"Well—it's just that we planned to do the master gardening classes. And we've got other projects where I'm going to need the family's help." He suddenly felt clammy and moved away from the air-conditioner.

"Yeah," she answered casually, "we'll have to do something about that. Carter's already said he's going to work at McDonald's, and Logan's just not into this."

"Obviously." He swallowed hard as he heard the bitter sarcasm creep into his own voice.

"Hey, look." Her tone jolted him, made him realize the resolve now entrenched in those eyes. "We've all got our own lives, you know. This is a big chance for me."

Thunder jarred the room as the lights dimmed, then flickered on again. Sheets of rain pounded against the windows.

"Do what you want," he snapped.

"I will! You can be sure of it." She turned to go, then stopped. "But don't you worry about your precious plans. We won't leave you out on a limb. You know better than that."

Defiantly, she grabbed her keys, strode to the door, and opened it. "We'll–" she had to shout to be heard above the rain–"We'll cover the bases here for you somehow. You'll see."

He was too stunned to go to the window to make sure she'd reached her car through the downpour. What in the hell, he wondered, did she mean by that?

Doris

October

She could have cried when she first saw Marty. Just sat right down and bawled at the sight of Kate's once-athletic husband hunched over his walker as he inched his way through the living room to greet Rosie and her. The Parkinson's was whipping him worse than any basketball opponent ever had when he'd been an Indiana high-school legend. A smile like pale sunshine broke through his blank expression as she met him and gave him a hug. God, she thought, inside his Notre Dame polo shirt he was a shaky rack of bones.

"It's been too long." Awkwardly she searched for the right words. "Still cheering for the Irish, I see." She nodded toward the gold logo embroidered on his navy shirt.

"Play like a champion," he replied, lifting his frail arm and pumping his fist before turning to greet Rosie.

Marveling that his spirit was still intact, Doris sagged into a relieved hug, first with Kate and then Cheryl. A quick glance assured her they hadn't changed much since she'd seen them at her house the year before. Oh, there might be a few more worry lines on Kate's face and a bit of weariness that she'd never noticed before in Cheryl. But here they were, the "Fearsome Four," together again. Kate motioned for them to find a chair and said she'd bring in some iced tea, while Marty shuffled toward a room down the hall.

Although it was the first time they'd ever gathered in South Bend, they'd agreed to come to Kate's house for lunch so she wouldn't have to get someone to stay all day with Marty. Cheryl had told them she'd take the South Shore train. Driving in unfamiliar territory made her nervous. Doris had picked up Rosie at her condo near Kankakee, and they hadn't stopped talking during the whole two-hour trip.

From the moment they'd turned onto Kate's shaded street, Doris had spotted the house right off. She'd have been able to pick it out of a lineup if she'd had to. It was just so Kate, so classy. Doris thought they called that style "Tudor." Whatever it was though, the place had been lived in hard and could use a little touching up.

"Geez, this is where Kevin rode his bike out in front of the car." Rosie's quiet observation had given Doris goosebumps as they drove up the steep driveway.

They'd exchanged a glance of mutual understanding, acknowledging the accident years ago that had made a life-changing impact on Kate's youngest child as well as her entire family.

Now, settling into the cushion of a roomy chair after the first rush of hugs, Doris heaved a happy sigh. Once more, she was in the company of her oldest friends. Once more, she could set down her burdens and melt into that comfortable spot she occupied with the Fearsome Four. Being with them was like sliding into her favorite pair of worn slippers.

For the first time, she glanced around the room. If the outside of the house reflected Kate, the inside was a dead giveaway. There were books everywhere. Trying not to stare, she noticed that the two floor-to-ceiling sets of shelves were stuffed. Paperbacks cluttered the end tables and were piled in uneven stacks on the floor at the end of the couch. Oh my God, she thought to herself, there must be as many books here as in the whole Rockwell library!

When she went to the kitchen to help Kate, she found more books—and not cookbooks, either. She helped Kate scoop chicken salad onto each plate and filled little bowls with fresh fruit.

"I bought the best rolls at one of the local bakeries, but I made the salad." Kate seemed to need to assure Doris that she'd tried to present a nice lunch. "You know cooking was never my strong suit. But I did do one more thing. Look."

She lifted the dome of a china pedestal to reveal a slightly lopsided layer cake. Doris realized that the uneven white frosting topped with colored sprinkles camouflaged some of the gaps. Still, she was touched that Kate had gone to the trouble to re-create a dessert they'd all remember.

"It's just like the ones your mom used to make." Doris recalled the unsettling envy she'd felt at Kate's birthday parties when Mrs. Freeman had unveiled one of her special cakes that looked like it had come straight from the Grab-It-Here. How Doris had wished her own mom could stay home from her factory job and turn out something fancier than a plain cake in a flat pan.

"Yep," Kate's pride showed in her voice. "Three layers. The top and bottom are pink and the middle one white, just like the old days. I had to celebrate your visit somehow." Carefully, she replaced the lid. "Do you realize how hard it was to keep Marty out of it?"

Doris chuckled, at the same time wondering how Kate could create much of anything in this old-timey kitchen with its small sink and aging stove. Most of the counter tops were covered with—she had to smile—more books. Well, she thought affectionately, Kate was, after all, a writer, not a caterer. This kitchen was just right for her.

Gathered around Kate's dining room table, the group attacked the food.

"Great chicken salad, Kate!" Cheryl's compliment was from the heart. "And you know I eat at lots of luncheons." Her brown eyes reflected her appreciation.

"I'm just glad people can't buy this in Rockwell," Doris added. "It'd give me 'n my girls a run for our money!" Silently, she scolded herself for thinking it might contain a tad too much mayo and could use a dash of something else. Dill, maybe?

As they eased into their old conversational routines, they covered—as always—the day they'd bonded when they'd escaped from the hobos and the memories they shared of the best and worst days of their lives. This part of their reunions was a ritual. When Kate brought out the cake and served it, they crowed with delight.

"Do you realize how jealous I always was of you and your birthday cakes?" Cheryl's silver bangles clattered on her wrist as she spoke. "You know, Lila thought she was going all out if she stuck a candle in a Twinkie for me."

They all smiled as they pictured Cheryl's mom painting her nails and tipping her glass half-filled with a dark amber liquid a little too often.

"We did well to keep a pan of brownies at our house," Rosie added. "Mom'd put 'em out to cool, and that Mike'd come through the kitchen and cut a big slab for himself. Right out of the center."

The mention of Mike's name brought a bittersweet silence, as each of the four recalled Rosie's mischievous younger brother who'd died on the train trestle when they were in eighth grade.

Kate pierced their reflective mood.

"I'll show you the rest of the house—the den where Marty spends most of his time and the three bedrooms upstairs. Then I thought you'd all like to see the Notre Dame campus," she suggested brightly. "One of Marty's old buddies from the *Trib* is going to stop by in a few minutes to keep him company while we're gone."

God, Doris thought. Kate really's got herself a job here, round the clock. No wonder her conversation seemed so cheerful, while the lines around her mouth looked deeper. Under her brave exterior, her old friend was carrying a heavy load. Doris wished she lived closer and could bring her a meal once in awhile.

After Kate ushered in Marty's friend and had seen they were all set with the golf channel in the little den, the four piled into her aging Volvo.

"In some ways, South Bend's not a whole lot different from Rockwell. Just bigger," Kate explained as she wound her way through her neighborhood at the edge of the campus. "A few more motels and restaurants and, of course, Notre Dame."

"Geez!" Rosie pointed ahead. "Now that's something you don't see every day."

Doris sucked in her breath. At the end of the street, against a sky the color of wild bachelor buttons, stood a building that looked like it was straight off a postcard. She squinted. The top must be made of pure gold! In some ways, she thought it was even more impressive than the Empire State Building she and her mom had toured several years ago when they'd gone to hear her brother Tommy play the piano in a New York hotel, before he'd been struck down with AIDS.

"Yeah, the fabled dome," Kate answered nonchalantly. "We'll park here at the bookstore, then walk up to the main building. The Basilica of the Sacred Heart's right there, and I know you'll want to see it."

Doris felt like they were moseying through a movie set as they crunched through the orange leaves that blanketed the campus sidewalks. She couldn't help but notice that the buildings seemed in perfect shape. As hard as she tried, she couldn't tell which were brand new and which were really old. The students who stepped into the grass to allow them to pass wore flip-flops and raggedy shirts that might have come from thrift stores. Still, Doris thought as she sized them up, these kids had the look of money. She bet a lot of them had even more than Alan had left her boys.

"I sure wish I could've brought Bud here before he died." Rosie seemed to be talking more to herself than to the rest of them. "I don't know why we didn't come."

As they quieted themselves and stepped up to enter Sacred Heart, Doris noticed Kate wince. She seemed to be favoring her left knee. Damn arthritis is probably bugging her, like everybody else, she thought.

A feeling of reverence washed over her as they stood for a moment, admiring the magnificence of the Basilica. It was a crying shame that her mom never saw this place! It had to be holy ground, for sure.

They listened with awe as Kate explained in a hushed voice the building's history and the story of its French stained glass windows. She told them to wander a bit on their own so they could drink in the beauty, then said they'd return to the bookstore.

"I know how you all like to shop." Her warm hazel eyes rested on each of them. "We'll have fun there, then I'll drive you on a loop of the campus so you can see the rest."

"Too far to walk?" Cheryl wondered.

"'Tis for me," Kate murmured.

As they left the hallowed atmosphere of the Basilica and stepped back into the autumn sunshine, Kate continued her explanation.

"I'm headed for a knee replacement right after Christmas."

"Geez!" Rosie scolded her. "You shoulda told us. We wouldn't have had to walk this far."

"How will you manage—I mean, with Marty and every-thing?" Cheryl hooked her arm into Kate's as they retraced their steps.

"Kevin and Lissa and their kids are coming before Christmas. Their two daughters will spend some time with college friends in Chicago while Kevin and his wife look after us." She held the bookstore door open for them. "Kev says he owes me some 'leg time' after all the care I gave him when he was growing up."

Although Doris smiled at this bit of dark humor, she could see the shadows flit across Kate's eyes. Her friend was scared but trying not to show it.

Inside the bookstore, the group scattered. Cheryl drifted toward the music section, while Kate couldn't keep herself out of the shelves displaying the latest fiction. Doris tagged along with Rosie, who wanted to buy a cap that Bud would have liked. Bored with Rosie's indecision, she idly picked up some stuffed animals. Violet might get a kick out of this tiny leprechaun, she thought, until she saw the $24.95 price tag and immediately placed it back on the display rack.

After they'd loaded themselves back into the car, Kate told them there was a funky little place named Lula's near the campus where they could grab a cup of coffee.

"If it's all the same with you, I'd just as soon go back to your house and have another piece of that cake before we head home." Rosie's talent for speaking her mind was one thing that had not changed over the years. Doris grinned at her honest request.

"You got it!" Obviously flattered that her baking efforts had been appreciated, Kate eased her car away from the campus and pointed it toward home.

"I can't stay forever," Cheryl reminded them. "I need a ride back to the station to catch the train in about an hour and a half."

"Consider it done," Doris volunteered. "We'll drop you

off on our way out of town—if Kate can give us the right directions." They all snickered, recalling how Kate—as smart as she was—had always had to ask for help whenever she went somewhere.

Back at the house they peeked in on Marty and found him dozing, while his friend thumbed through several sports magazines.

"Hey, Kate—okay if I make some coffee?" Doris knew she'd be struggling to stay awake for the drive home if she didn't get some caffeine into her. "Let's just sit around your kitchen table."

"Okay to both." Kate concentrated as she lifted slabs of cake onto the mismatched plates that she took from the cupboard. "I've given you one meal in the dining room. From here on out, we'll just wing it." She grimaced as she lowered herself onto her chair.

Rosie stabbed a hearty bite of cake, stuffed it into her mouth, and didn't wait before she began to talk.

"I sure wish the kids at Colton's school looked more like the ones we just saw."

"But he's in art school and–" Kate jumped in to protect the kid who'd been like Rosie's own since she'd started tutoring him in third grade.

"I know, I know." Rosie rubbed her left eye to keep it from twitching. "But his mom's on chemo now for ovarian cancer. I love her like a sister, but she's not gonna be much good to him. At least for awhile."

They waited silently as Rosie took another bite.

"You know, he's got this cutie-patootie girlfriend." She waved her fork and rolled her eyes. "But he doesn't need more distractions. He needs to finish school and get a job."

"Could be a rough ride for awhile. I've been there, done that." Cheryl was somber as she spoke. "Think of the crazy stunts I pulled. Life in the arts isn't the best road to security."

"Well, you did okay though," Doris assured her. "You and Jarvis found each other, even if you weren't together long enough. You're—you're on solid ground now and you've got your nice apartment."

Doris stopped. Why in hell did she feel she'd said something wrong? Cheryl squirmed.

"That's the one thing I wanted to tell you today," she said. "I'm moving. Next month."

They all fell silent, too stunned to respond.

"I've decided to go into an assisted living place." Cheryl sipped her coffee as they waited for her to continue. "I've got some macular degeneration going on, and I want to get set up in a spot where I'll have a support system when I need it."

"Oh." Kate's response was one word, but Doris knew it meant that Kate suddenly realized how grateful she was that she and Marty had their kids to help them. Cheryl didn't have that luxury.

"It's—it's a lovely place. In Evanston." Cheryl's voice broke. "I'm lucky that Jarvis left me with enough for this kind of thing. Can you imagine the dump I'd be living in today if I'd stayed married to Rip?"

Doris snickered as they all relaxed at the mention of Cheryl's good-for-nothing second husband.

"Lordy, I know. It may be premature." Cheryl swished her hair and flashed her sunniest smile. "But in a way, I'll be a pioneer for all of us. The first of the Fearless Four to charge into assisted living!" Her voice quivered. "Besides, that mean old Loneliness that's bugged me all my life keeps hanging around. In the shadows, I feel it. Maybe–maybe it'll be better for me to live where there's people. And stuff going on."

At the sight of Cheryl's false courage, Doris knew she had to say something.

"You're not alone. We're goin' to have to do somethin' about Violet before long. She's in way worse shape than any of us." There. She'd stated the biggest fear on her mind. "Half the time she's all mixed up. Last week I came home and found she'd fixed supper for all my kids and couldn't figure out why they didn't come home from school." Biting her lip to keep it steady, she realized she needed to get out of there before she fell apart.

"Hey," she elbowed Cheryl, "we'd better be headin' for that train station."

"But we haven't even talked about your family!" Cheryl glanced at her watch. "Give us a quick rundown."

"Long story short: The girls and David are doin' good." Doris counted down on her fingers, as she always did when she talked about her kids. "Dirk's business is growing every day, but I'm worried that he's workin' his family too hard— kinda like Bill did me. I've warned him about it—hope he listens to me more'n Dougie ever does. That's about it."

Whew, that kitchen sure seemed hot! She patted her face and put her napkin on the table.

"And Denny?" Kate's question hung in the air like a small black cloud.

"Same old, same old. I—I can't–" Feeling swallowed up by the topic of Denny, she pushed back her chair and headed blindly for the nearest bathroom. After she'd closed the door, she took a few deep breaths and splashed cold water on her cheeks.

"Damn you, Denny," she whispered as she wondered why some old wounds seemed to get worse as the years went by. Then she peered at the reflection of her steady gray eyes in the mirror.

"Get it together, Doris," she ordered. Trying to cloak herself in the confidence that she wore as the one in charge at The Boulder, she opened the bathroom door.

"Okay, girls, taxi's leavin'," she called, hoping her voice sounded stronger than she felt. "Let's go. We don't want Cheryl to miss that train!"

2007

Dirk

March

Where <u>was</u> the sunshine this year? As he watched the leaden snowflakes plop on the panes of his weatherbeaten greenhouse, Dirk wondered if March might be the meanest month of all. For as long as he could remember, an early spring Saturday morning had been an open invitation to carve out narrow trenches in his garden plot where he could scatter seeds for his peas, radishes, and lettuce. This year, however, he knew his back yard would have to take a back seat to his business. He prayed his customers would snap up every bit of all that pond equipment he'd splurged on.

Kicking a sprinkling can in frustration, he sighed as the tinny sound reverberated, then faded. How could this building that had nurtured such hope and fulfillment in him last spring have morphed into a cave of loneliness that bordered on despair in one year?

He knew <u>he</u> wasn't the one to blame. That much was sure. Dragging two sealed crates from a dusty corner, he pried them open and began to extract the shipment of new ceramic urns.

His family had deserted him. That's what happened. Carter had signed up for another shift at McDonald's. The pay was decent, but the kid had also found he enjoyed the attention he received from some of the upper-class girls who liked to hang out there and tease him. Dirk made a mental note to warn him about their cunning tactics.

Logan was training in the school gym with the track team and would be distracted until summer. Dirk tried to convince himself that at least his boys were involved in worthwhile projects, but he couldn't shake his disappointment at not having them toiling alongside him every minute. After all, that had been his dream when he'd bought this business.

Then there was the matter of the second greenhouse. He and Doug hadn't finished securing the last pane of glass before he'd discovered they'd created even more work to be done. And fewer family members to help, he realized glumly. It sure was weird how getting what he'd wanted had brought him down this thorny path.

Taking a deep breath, he inhaled the moist, earthy air that Darcy had always said smelled like worms but had always carried such comfort to him. Not today though. In previous years when March rolled around, he'd allowed his mind to wander to the golf league as he anticipated peaceful, long-shadowed evenings on the course with Ben. But last week Ben had broken the news that there'd be little golf for him in the summer ahead. After he'd survived a merger with Chicagoland National, Ben would have little time to dwell on chips and putts. He said he'd have to crank up his work ethic just to keep up with the accelerated pace—and at half his former salary.

Shoot, Dirk realized, two of the twelve urns in the first crate were damaged and would have to be returned. He slammed his fist into the box in disgust. His whole life seemed to have a crack in it right now.

Worst of all was the empty feeling he had when he thought about his wife.

"What the hell's going on with Nora?" his mom had asked last week. "She hardly shows up for anything any-more—even when I've baked a coconut cream pie."

He'd like an answer to that question himself. Lately their lives seemed to be running on automatic pilot. Often she'd call him on his cell to tell him she was going to stay in Danville between an afternoon class and an evening meeting of the county Democrats. Because she'd immersed herself in promotional efforts on behalf of their Illinois senator, Barack Obama, she'd babble on about his possible chances of being nominated for president the next year. But by the time she got home, Dirk would be snoring, and she'd slip silently into her side of the bed without waking him.

He didn't mind that he'd learned to use the crock pot to save money on meals for the boys and him, but he sure did miss his time alone with Nora at the end of each day. He couldn't remember the last time they'd had sex. And that he did care about.

Grateful that the second crate of urns held no damaged goods, he recalled Nora's odd promise when they'd argued last fall: "We'll cover the bases for you." He still didn't know what she'd meant by that. Nobody from his family had showed up to help him today, a Saturday morning, when everyone should have been here.

He felt his stomach growl as he groped through the packing papers and grabbed the return slip. Maybe he'd run over to McDonald's and let Carter fix him a Big Mac for lunch. He didn't think he could face a plate of last night's leftover slow-cooked chicken.

Slamming the chipped urns back into the box, he swore silently under his breath. As he grumbled that he shouldn't have to waste his valuable time packing up damaged goods to return to the wholesaler, he heard a noise from the office. He hoped it wasn't a rat.

"Anybody here?" An unfamiliar female voice repeated the question as he brushed his hands on his jeans and hustled toward the front. Maybe someone had stopped to ask directions. Nobody would have come in to do business on a morning in March.

"Yeah. Out here." he answered. "I'll be right in."

Before he could make his way through the greenhouse, the visitor appeared in the doorway.

"You Dirk?"

He rubbed his eyes to make sure he wasn't hallucinating. There stood a twenty-something dish, dressed in the most outlandish outfit he'd ever seen. His first glance showed that the husky voice came from a petite babe with green eye shadow and a tangle of spiky black hair highlighted with a bleached blond strip that started over her left eye. Her huge gold earrings swung as she strutted toward him. He was sure no one in Rockwell owned a neon patchwork jacket like hers.

"Yeah." Stepping around the planting tables, he realized her turquoise skin-tight pants stopped just short of her laced-up gold sandals. Sandals in March? Who wore something like that?

"Nora said you could use some help." She thrust out her hand and scanned the greenhouse. "No offense, but looks like she was right. I'm Gina Corletti. Me 'n her met at the school cafeteria. I'm cashier there. That job sucks, so I can spare a few hours to pitch in." Popping her gum, she stopped talking long enough to size him up, from his scuffed shoes to the gray streak in his hair. "If you want me, that is."

He sensed energy behind those lively brown eyes–more energy than he'd felt in a long time. Feeling the firmness of her grip, he realized that Nora had lived up to her promise. She really was trying to cover the bases for him. But with this goofy statement of fashion? He wasn't sure.

She giggled as his stomach groaned again.

"I need some lunch." He smiled sheepishly. "Let's talk about it over a burger."

"I could use a decent sandwich." Her words were muffled behind her wad of gum. "Nora says your mom runs a pretty good diner."

As he reached for his windbreaker, he wasn't convinced he wanted to subject this little whirl of color to the scrutiny of everyone at The Boulder. On the other hand, he didn't want to eat lunch under Carter's questioning eye at McDonald's.

"Mom's it is," he agreed, pulling the greenhouse door shut behind him and motioning toward his truck.

"Hey, a Ford F-150!" Her voice was full of admiration as she hoisted herself onto the seat. "My old boyfriend used to have one of these. Until the repo guy took it away." A sharp pop from her gum signaled the end of that topic.

Misgivings filled him as he drove through town to The Boulder. He wondered who'd be working today. Maybe he should've settled for Carter's icy gaze at McDonald's. One thing was sure: He didn't have to worry about making conversation. This Gina girl was a non-stop monologue.

"Only been to Rockwell twice in my life. Too small for me. No night life." Pop! Pop! "When I get sick of Danville, I head for Champaign." Pop! "You hear what I'm sayin'?"

"My sister lives there–" he offered.

"I kinda like the funky college places." She paused. "Kinda like some of the funky college boys too."

"Yeah–"

"A lot more stuff to do in Champaign. Movies. Night life. You like movies?"

"I haven't been to–"

"Me 'n my girlfriend went to see 'Failure to Launch' at the dollar show. Golly, gee—we're here already? Like I said, there's not much to Rockwell."

He wondered how he could be both drained and exhilarated by the time he found himself following her gaudy jacket into the restaurant. How could Nora expect him to get any work out of somebody like this? This woman had the worst case of diarrhea mouth he'd ever seen.

He felt more settled the minute he opened the door and the soothing aroma of his mom's familiar comfort food greeted him. He'd never been able to pinpoint that distinctive mix—maybe the lingering effects of pancakes and fried potatoes from breakfast, mingled with the simmering kettle of homemade chicken-and-dumpling soup. He'd loved that smell since he was the little kid who felt so important when he filled the catsup bottles and wiped off the salt and pepper shakers at each table.

As he guided Gina to one of the two back booths where family members always congregated, he recalled how everyone had pitched in back then to make sure Mom got her work done. Well, everyone but Denny. Debbie'd learned enough business basics to help her launch her beauty shops in Champaign, and Darcy'd become their mom's right hand in the kitchen. David had been wise enough to spot opportunities for the restaurant to grow and improve, while Dirk and Doug had just done as they'd been told, cleaning tables, washing dishes, and prepping vegetables for salads. Mom had figured it all out, how to make their family a team. Why couldn't he do the same with his greenhouses?

Gina gave him a thumbs up as they scooted into one of the signature royal blue booths.

"Better'n McDonald's." Pop! "I can see that already." She drummed the table with her fingers to Kenny Chesney's "When the Sun Goes Down" with such verve that other customers began to glance at her. He supposed it was too late to go somewhere else.

"At supper time every night they play some of my Uncle Tommy's CDs. Just for an hour." He sat up straighter. "I like that time best," he confided.

"Yeah?" Showing little interest, she cracked her gum loudly and craned her neck so she could study a couple in the booth across from them.

"He was a famous pianist in New York City. My mom's brother. Tommy Panczyk."

Her blank expression indicated she neither knew nor

cared about his uncle.

"No offense, but do they play any Clay Aiken. Or Fergie? You know, something new."

"Hey, Uncle Dirk." He was relieved when Darcy's daughter, Tiffany, appeared. She placed two small plates and a basket of rolls in front of them, then pulled laminated sheets from under her arm.

"Look," his niece continued without taking a breath, "we got new menus. Finally! I told Grandma we needed some heart-healthy choices, and she actually listened to me. Just about kills her to substitute light ingredients for the real stuff, but she knows we've gotta keep up with the latest food fads."

"Yeah. Nice." Scanning the new options centered in a pale pink heart in the middle of the menu, he said, "Mom was smart to add those southwestern dishes a few years ago too."

Tiffany nodded. "But no pizza! She'll never do pizza."

He snickered. "Barley's turf, right?"

"Right. Hey, you taking a friend to lunch?" Her brown pony tail swished as she glanced at Gina and stated the obvious with her usual frankness, "You don't look like Nora."

"You're pretty observant." He felt his face reddening as he made a feeble effort to skirt the issue with dry wit. "This is Gina." He fixed his gaze directly on Tiffany. "Nora sent her up from Danville to see if she could put in a few hours at the greenhouse."

He watched as the two subtly evaluated each other with one brief sweeping glance.

"Glad you're here." Tiffany's welcoming smile was

genuine. "God knows Uncle Dirk could use some help. Hey, we got some killer onion rings you might like."

"You're on." Gina shoved the menu back at her. "And bring me one of them pork tenderloins like that guy's got over there, some slaw, and some baked beans. None of that light stuff you mentioned." She parked her gum on the small plate in front of her. "I'll hold off on dessert till I finish the first round."

He relaxed as Tiffany telegraphed a look that conveyed the message, I bet you didn't know you were going to have to pay for all this.

"Uncle Dirk's a <u>big</u> spender," his niece answered face-tiously. "He'll buy you as much dessert as you can put away."

Ignoring Tiffany's playful sarcasm, he asked, "Your mom or grandma working today?"

"Nope, they're catering a big party. I'm it today, so you're stuck with the B team."

As she gave him an understanding wink, he knew in his heart that Tiffany felt his relief. He wasn't sure he was ready for this little firecracker sitting across from him to invade his greenhouse, let alone have to answer questions from his mom or his sister.

Testing the waters, he gnawed at his burger and outlined the help he'd need at the greenhouse and the hours he'd expect her to work. She listened, nodded, and chewed, silently devouring the mountain of food in front of her.

"The pay wouldn't be that much–" He hated to approach the subject of an hourly wage.

"Apple pie. Ala mode," Gina called out to Tiffany across the room. Those were the only words she uttered throughout the entire meal.

Good grief, Dirk realized, if she can work as efficiently as she can eat, I think I've got a keeper here.

Gina picked up a toothpick, while he paid their bill and waved good-bye to Tiffany. As they stepped into the pale spring sunshine, he felt the morning gloom lifting from his shoulders. Humming Kenny Chesney's catchy melody that had played several times during lunch, he watched as Gina nimbly lifted herself into his truck.

He grinned as he opened his own door and heard the distinctive signature of her presence.

Pop!

Maybe the coming season wasn't going to be as bleak as he'd first thought.

Doug

July

"Be careful with them food baskets, Dougie." The edge in his mother's voice as she stood rooted to the pier said it all. "Be sure you put that cold stuff where the sun won't hit it."

"No problem, Mom."

He knew she'd always had a tendency to get bossy when she was unsure of herself. He handed the baskets to Maria and reminded her to put the salads and deviled eggs in the fridge. Then he extended his arm and started the challenging task of loading his mother onto the boat. If it hadn't been for his older brother, David, now guiding her into position, none of them would be heading out on this overcast morning.

"No way, Dougie!" his mom had replied a few days ago when they'd shared a big meal at her house and welcomed David home from Atlanta for his annual visit. His wife, SueBeth, had stayed home to manage a community health fair and keep an eye on their two teenage daughters.

It'd never bothered Doug that everyone in the family

adored David, his mom's pride-and-joy success story. Well, everyone but Denny, who still showed traces of the childish jealousy he'd carried all these years. Denny'd always resented the fact that everything in school had come so easy for David, while he himself had struggled to maintain average grades.

But David, so relaxed and unassuming as he'd bitten into their mother's fried chicken at that family supper, had played the trump card when they discussed the boat.

"How do you know you won't like it, Mom, if you don't try?"

There. Just like that, David had turned the tables when he delivered one of her own favorite motivators in a tone softened by the southern location where he'd lived for several years His fine features, graced by his gray eyes, looked like a picture of their Uncle Tommy back when he'd been healthy.

Their mom had attempted a few excuses before she'd finally given in to David.

"Well, maybe this once. I've gotta die of something." Her face had hardened with resolve. "And just a short day trip. You're not gettin' me on that thing overnight. I want to be off it before dark."

Now, with Maria, Cherisse, and his sisters Debbie and Darcy already aboard, they were almost ready to glide away from the marina. Dirk had said he couldn't afford to leave the greenhouse for an entire day, and Denny'd made up some excuse about having to see a guy about a used tractor. At least, Doug could give his mom a day with four of her kids plus a granddaughter.

Her arm trembled as she tentatively placed one foot on

the back seat of the "Windfall."

"Hell, Dougie, I can't do this. The damn thing's bouncin' all over." Grimacing, she began to pull her foot out of the boat as it bobbed in the waves.

"Sure you can, Mom. David's right there behind you. Just pick up your other leg and you're in." They'd come this far, he thought. He wasn't going to let her chicken out now.

Beads of sweat covered her face as she straddled the boat, unable to propel herself over its edge.

"Here we go, Mom." Gently, David lifted her leg over the side of the boat. "Ahoy, matey!" He flashed a triumphant grin at Doug.

Knowing they shouldn't rush her, Doug eased her into the seat and let her catch her breath.

"Way to go, Mom. Nothing to it." He nodded in appreciation to David, who hopped in beside their mother and began to untie the ropes anchoring them to the pier.

Gulping shallow breaths, she grumbled, "God never meant for me to ride in no boat."

The quick look that David gave him conveyed the message that this could be a long afternoon. He was grateful when the girls came to his rescue.

"Hey, Mom," Darcy held out her hand, "you've gotta see this cute little kitchen. You'll never believe it. Plus, we could use some help with the food." She steadied their mother on one side, while Debbie shored up the other. Reluctantly their mom tottered toward the galley.

My sisters are something else, Doug thought to himself. They know that's the one place where Mom'll feel comfortable. Hauling in the ropes that David tossed him, he curled them on the floor, then, from his spot in the captain's seat, steered them away from the pier.

David couldn't contain his admiration as they churned through the bay on their way to the lake. Exclaiming over the beauty of the interior, the smooth ride, and the general ambiance of the boat, he made Doug feel like an admiral as he stood at the helm of the "Windfall."

"Alan would have loved this," David told him. "More than anybody. Even you. Wow! Look at the view of that skyline!"

"I bet I know someone who might've liked it even better'n Alan," Doug answered.

David cocked his head and rubbed his chin.

"I give up," he conceded. "Who?"

"Spud," Doug said. "Old Spud. The guy who taught us so much stuff. I think he'd have liked a ride like this."

"He sure would. He sure would." David reflected for a moment. "I remember the time when I was a little kid and he showed me how to fix the sump pump. I almost popped out of my britches, I was so proud."

"Yep, I wish we coulda brought him along." Doug turned the wheel to steer them up the shoreline. "But not–"

"Aunt Violet." They finished the sentence in unison, then laughed so hard they almost fell out of their seats. While the wind ruffled his hair and the sun warmed his face, Doug soaked up a moment of satisfaction deeper than any he'd felt since he'd first bought the boat. Lately he'd wondered if friends and acquaintances had come to take his hospitality for granted. The thrill of sailing the "Windfall" had often been replaced with the burden of making sure he and Maria didn't forget to invite someone and—worse yet—paying all the bills.

But not this day. Still convulsing with David over their mutual mental picture of stubborn Aunt Violet, he glanced at his mom. She seemed to be settling in.

"Don't you boys get to actin' silly up there!" she yelled. "Somebody's gotta run this thing. Are you dead sure there's no rain in those clouds?"

"Not a drop," he called as he motioned for David to take over at the wheel. Slipping into the seat across from his brother, he scooped up Cherisse and hugged her. Today, Maria had made one fat braid of his granddaughter's black hair and coiled it into a bun. Stray wisps tickled his chin as she bounced on his lap.

This has gotta be a little slice of heaven, he thought as he watched weeks of tension slide from David's shoulders. Even his brother's well-cut hair seemed to relax in the wind.

"Go lead-foot, Uncle David!" Cherisse shouted over the roar of the engines.

"Not yet, honey." Doug shook his head. "Grand-do's kinda scared."

"Scared?" Cherisse turned and fixed her gray eyes on him. "Why?"

"She's never been on a boat before. She's spent all her time working."

"Can this go as fast as Kevin Harvick's car?" Cherisse studied the length of the boat.

"Not wicked fast. Just fast." Doug smiled. Damned if his granddaughter couldn't be as pushy as his mom sometimes! No wonder Maria sometimes referred to her as "Little Doris."

Sliding from his lap, Cherisse made her way to his mother, cuddled up to her, and whispered in her ear. When his mom made a face, Cherisse made two more appeals before she could coax a nod of agreement from her great-grandmother.

Immediately, a triumphant Cherisse approached David with firm directions, then returned to Doug's lap. He watched with pride as David gave the lever a shove and felt the surge of power, but cringed when he saw his mom's knuckles whiten as she gripped her seat. Skimming the water with grace and speed, the boat left the skyline in the distance and approached the north shore buildings he'd learned to recognize.

Cherisse whooped with the thrill of her accomplishment. As Debbie and Darcy giggled in the mist that showered them, he realized, "This is it! This is why I bought the boat. This is what Alan wanted us to do—to have fun together as a family."

Things really seemed to be going good for him these days. He was grateful those ugly tussles over money with Renee weren't quite as frequent, now that she was seeing that guy named Brandon from Watseka.

Sighing contentedly, he smiled at the flush of pure joy on David's face. He loved it that his sisters were happy, that he'd given his big brother a good day, that Maria was having a terrific time.

Cherisse cheered and yelled, "Faster! Faster!" Even his mom wore a look of surprised wonder he'd never seen before.

"Don't feel you've gotta take this thing all the way to Canada," she shouted to David.

They all laughed as he slowed.

"Aw gee, Grand-do," Cherisse lamented. "Why'd you tell him that?"

"'Cause we gotta eat sometime," his mom barked, the color returning to her face. Still, he glimpsed a spirit in her eyes that he'd rarely seen since Alan died.

His mom relaxed as they devoured the food she and Darcy had prepared. Debbie had dressed up their fare with cute little unnecessary nautical napkins–so typically Debbie, he thought–and admitted she'd yearned for a day like this. Darcy added that she, too, had needed time off.

"Too bad Dirk couldn't come along." With her dark brown curls, Debbie still looked like the sister who had teased him every day of his life when they were growing up. He'd known from the way his dad had called her "Princess" that she was his favorite—well, other than Denny, who'd worked his butt off to please him.

"Our baby brother's got his hands full." Doug scooped a load of dip onto a potato chip and popped it into his mouth. "He's at the greenhouses morning, noon, and night."

"But the way I see it, he's not all work and no play. Everyone says he's got that hot little helper from Danville out there most days." Debbie's words hung in the air like a threatening cloud. "That's probably the real reason he's not here."

Doug lifted his bottle of Budweiser, then stopped and stared at Debbie. She'd always protected Dirk when they were little, but now she was using the same judgmental tone to dis their younger brother that she'd always reserved for Doug when he'd pulled one of his antics. What the hell?

136

"Naw, he's in over his head." He stabbed a deviled egg. "Have you seen all that pond stuff he's still got in stock?"

"Nope." Debbie tipped her own bottle of Bud. "But I've seen that girl. What's her name, Gina? I've seen her snuggled up to some of the U of I football players in bars around Champaign." Behind Debbie's winsome smile, Doug could sense some fierceness starting to surface.

He glanced at Maria and caught the wary look in her eyes.

"Well, he sure needs–" Darcy spoke up.

"He needs his wife is what he needs," their mom interrupted. "Even Nick's settled down since he married that nice Amy last winter. But the woman Dirk's got workin' for him's a fart in the wind. Reminds me of your Tonya, Dougie." Using a crust of her homemade bread, she soaked up the remaining sauce from the baked beans. "And that ain't good."

"Grand-do, we're not s'posed to say 'ain't.'" Cherisse's observation made them laugh but couldn't quite break the tension that had built among them.

"Hey, Dougie, there's clouds over there!" The depth of his mom's alarm startled all of them. "We'd better head back before we get rained on."

"We're already wet, Grand-do." Once again, Cherisse dropped a gem of wisdom.

As they sped along the skyline, they continued to fret about Dirk and indulge in their longtime resentment of the unnecessary pain Denny had caused them. Once they'd aired their feelings, however, they gave way to memories—the stack of stories that they alone shared.

"Remember our first day at Sweet Briar?"

"Remember when we switched Aunt Violet's sugar and salt on April Fool's Day and Spud spanked every one of us?"

"Remember your sweet shot from the corner that won us so many games, Doug?"

"The one that Uncle Charley taught me," he recalled.

Once they had docked and his mom stood secure on the pier again, Maria gave him a high five.

"Way to go, kochany." The promising smile in her eyes said it all.

"Yep, we Polish sure know how to have a good time!" He wasn't sure if it was bliss or relief he heard in his mom's voice. He only knew she seemed happy and that she loved to hear Maria use the old-world expressions she'd learned as a child.

He wondered if he should go to mass tomorrow, just to give thanks for such a great day.

Doris

August

*H*ey it's me again & the three of you won't never believe
what I did a few days ago.

Get yourselves a cup of coffee and sit down, cuz this will
be kinda long. But I cant wait til we get together in Oct. to
tell you about it and I dont wanna make 3 phone calls.

I went out on Dougie's boat!!! Me—ol scaredy cat Doris!

Davids here and sweet talked me into it. Honest to God.
Dougie and Maria asked all my kids, but Dirk is to busy and
Denny—well you know Denny. But Debbie came over for the
day and Darcy and me fixed a lunch for everybody. Cherisse
went along to.

I tried not to show I was scared shitless. Just climing into
that thing took 10 years off my life. But Dougie drove real
careful cuz of me. Cherisse got David to go super fast but
not for long.

I felt like I was riding thru a picture painting if you know
what I mean. Chicago was on one side and the big ol huge
lake everywhere else. I tried not to think about all that water.

We laughed a lot. God, that felt good to laugh like that with four of my kids. If I have to get in a boat to have that again, Ill do it. We talked about old times when they was growing up. I wish Denny wouldve come. We all did but then you know how moody he can be.

We missed our baby, Dirk. And we talked about his business. Its sucking the life out of him. I worry about that. My kids is all worried about the woman Nora sent to help him out. She makes me think of Dougie's Tonya. Only worse if posible. I gotta do something about that. I just don't know what.

I hope Alan woud be happy with how my boys used the money he left them. I thought the restrant business was risky but selling plants might be worse. And Im scared that Dougie will spend all his keeping that boat in the water.

I was scared to when the wind blew up some clouds and rocked the boat. But I didnt jump off. Ha Ha.

I hope Marty is doing good, KATE.

And I hope you still like your new place, CHERYL. Maybe we can see it next summer sometime.

ROSIE, we all will see you for lunch in Kankakee in a couple months, but Ill probly see you before then.

Love from your old friend whos still a scaredy cat. But Im working on it.

Doris

Dirk

October

He loved how the late-afternoon shadows seemed to swallow entire sections of the fairways, especially in the fall when the red and gold maples dotted the course with brilliant color.

He loved riding in the cart with Ben. Seated, his tall buddy didn't make him feel like such a pipsqueak, the way he did when they unloaded their clubs and walked through the pro shop.

What he did not like one bit were the disruptive images that crowded his mind every time Ben left the cart to eyeball the distance of his next drive. Dirk couldn't help but think of his mom. Lately, during her spare time, she'd been showing up at odd hours to help at the greenhouse. He hadn't liked her comparison of Gina to Tonya, and he sure hadn't liked the way she'd scrutinized Gina with looks that could wither the healthiest plants.

"Lord knows every business goes through growing pains," his mom had told him last week. "I sure had my share at The Boulder. Just be careful. With everything, Dirk-honey." She'd fired him one of her I'm-not-fooling glances. "With everything."

Ben groaned as he folded his lanky frame into the cart and headed toward Dirk's ball.

"Didn't hit it. Now it's too short for a drive to the hole, too long for a chip. I've gotta get somebody to help me work on my pitch shot," he chided himself.

Dirk said nothing as they stopped beside his ball. Sometimes silence was the best answer when a guy ranted about his poor play. He knew Ben had a lot of stuff on his mind, with the new demands that Chicagoland National was making of him.

He tugged a seven iron from his weathered bag, then replaced it with a five and sent the ball in a perfect arc straight to the green. That really felt good!

"Going for your personal best today?" Ben's gray hair tumbled over his forehead as he focused his wide grin on Dirk. "Nobody else around here's got the short game you have. Hell, I miss our league."

Dirk sank his putt for a birdie. Maybe he was on target for his best round ever. He'd never carded a par for eighteen holes. Maybe today was the day. He looked away as Ben's ball rimmed the cup and ricocheted to the left about six feet.

"We need to play more. At least I do." Ben sighed as he steered the cart to the tenth tee. "Been out in Doug's boat much this summer?"

Dirk studied the clumps of white birch trees that bordered the boundary all the way to the green. The grounds-keepers needed to do something about all those bag worms, he thought.

"Nope." He hit a three wood, long and straight. "Haven't been on it since right after he bought it. That was two years ago."

"He's never asked me." Ben connected solidly with his wood and put the ball within a few feet of Dirk's. "Ol' Doug and I were never the best of buddies, even when we played basketball together in high school. You know that. I wasn't quite in his league. In more ways than one."

"Yep. None of us could believe how fast he blew Alan's money. At least I invested mine in a business. Bought myself a ton of work though. <u>And</u> worry." As they bounced along the fairway, he tried to steer their conversation away from negative thoughts. "Doug's sure got a heckuva nice wife now."

"And that's a good thing," Ben agreed as he stopped along the cart path near the green. "I think God punished him double for every nasty trick he pulled as a kid when he gave him the sexy Miss Tonya for a wife."

Tonya. Now Dirk had to shove her image out of his head. His mom had actually compared Gina—cute, sweet, fun-loving, hard-working, gum-popping Gina—to the bitch Doug had married.

He never would have been able to get through the summer season without Gina. When Nora was able to help, she'd jumped right in and worked alongside Gina. The two women had cackled like schoolgirls as they'd deadheaded petunias and marigolds for their midsummer sale. Nora's moods, however, had been all over the place–wildly proud that her unusual flower selections had sold in a hurry, but shaken by concern that most of their pond equipment and upscale decorative items still gathered dust.

"It's the economy," he'd explained. "Things'll improve next year."

"They will if Obama gets elected." That was Nora's automatic cure-all for everything that was wrong these days—their struggling business, their apathetic sons, their passionless marriage.

"Sure hope he starts with Danville. People say they've never seen downtown so shabby." Pop! Gina had not stopped sprinkling the plants but punctuated her opinion with the sound of her gum.

Now he blinked hard to erase the image of Nora and Gina together, side by side, as he took a few practice swings with his nine iron. Then, with his mind momentarily cleared of distractions, he clipped the ball crisply and placed it two inches from the hole.

At the fourteenth, he guided his tee shot straight down the middle, but Ben hooked his into the woods. Ambling toward the green while Ben conducted a fruitless search for his ball, he once more felt the presence of the two women in his life. He had no control over either of them. He had to realize that. Nora still loved him but right now was swept away in her own cause. He'd never hurt her for the world.

But that jaunty little Gina was enough to make a guy crazy. During the last couple of months he'd dismissed all thoughts that she was coming on to him. It must have been an accident that her arm touched his when both of them were at the cash register, so close that the scent of her cologne had stirred feelings in him he didn't know he had. He'd given up on glancing away when she bent over in front of him in those tight pants she always wore and decided to enjoy the view. And last week, when he'd taken her with him to pick up a pizza at Barley's, he'd had a sense of pride when he saw how great she and his old buddy were getting along.

"How's tricks?" Barley had been his most charming. Rolling his unlit cigar around in his mouth, he'd ogled Gina. "You're sure not hurting for business." The way he'd said it had made Dirk realize that Barley'd been referring to Gina's hot looks.

"Not so great, actually." Dirk had pulled out a few bills, counted his money carefully, and placed it, complete with the right change, on the counter. "The economy. You know that, Barley."

"Yeah." Barley hadn't looked up as he'd swept Dirk's payment into the palm of his hand. "That's when you gotta start making adjustments to survive."

"Adjustments?" He'd been puzzled.

"Yeah, you know. Shave a little here, cut a little there. Hell, the customer never knows the difference."

Gina had snickered when he'd lifted the lid to inspect his pizza and found a full measure of the toppings he'd ordered.

"Guess you didn't do that to us." He'd given Barley a straight look. Gina had merely popped her gum and smiled.

"Never to you, my friend." Barley had stopped chewing on his cigar and squinted at him. "But don't ever forget you can bend the rules. Sometimes you have to if you're gonna survive." He'd winked at Gina, who had waved coyly to him.

By the time they'd returned to the greenhouse, he realized he'd lost his appetite when he'd opened the pizza box.

Sometimes a conversation with Barley could do that to a guy. Gina, however, had gobbled four slices, plus two of his beers to wash them down.

"Two holes to go," Ben now observed, shaking Dirk from his preoccupations as he teed up at the seventeenth. If he could nail this easy par four and bogey the next hole, he'd have his best round ever. He'd always been intimidated by the challenging eighteenth with its long dogleg left, its stream that wiggled across the fairway, and the pond to the right of the green.

Ben whistled as Dirk crushed the ball with his three wood, then followed with a perfect drive of his own.

"We'll to have to hustle if we're going to get in by dark. I hate it when the days are so short. Means winter's coming." Ben's hair flopped on his forehead as he floored the cart's pedal. "I'd sure rather be out here than down at the bank. The guys from Chicago are tightening the screws on us."

Dirk swallowed, ignoring the fact that he was two months behind with his loan payments. He needed to concentrate on his next shot.

"Banking's sure no fun anymore," Ben lamented as he stepped out to hit his ball.

"Been a tough year at the greenhouse, too." Satisfied with his eight iron, Dirk figured he could get his par with two putts. Zipping his windbreaker, he pulled the collar around his neck. Twilight dimmed the fall foliage to dull brown as the breeze carrying the promise of November nipped at him.

Two putts later he tried not to think about the bogey he needed at the final hole. Shoot, he realized, Ben was still dwelling on banking as he steered the cart down the fairway, venting about the new management's insistence that he do routine collateral evaluations.

"I'll be out sometime next week to do yours," Ben added as an afterthought.

In an attempt to avoid the woods on the left, Dirk aimed his tee shot to the right. It came to rest behind a knoll, the worst place for scooting around the dogleg. When he dubbed his next attempt, he knew he'd have to hit a layup to avoid landing in the stream.

Ben, on the other hand, seemed to benefit from having been able to air his frustrations about the poor small-business climate. He was actually down to the stream in two on this impossible hole.

Wishing his buddy would shut up for once, Dirk used too much club and pitched his ball to the far edge of the green. It fell softly, then seemed to make up its mind to trickle off. Still, he figured, one good chip and a solid putt and he'd get his personal best.

"Hey, don't listen to me." Ben scooped his ball out of the hole and held the flag. "I'll stop talking so you can hit."

Dirk's chip dribbled onto the green, leaving him a six-foot putt for his best round ever. Shoving the image of unsold merchandise and anemic income figures from his mind, he meticulously lined up his putt.

"Be careful, Dirk-honey." Once more he attempted to shake off the distracting advice his mom had given him. She'd known all about a floundering business—and she'd survived. So would he.

He breathed deeply, backed away from the ball, and took a second look. He needed to hit it squarely–not too hard and a little to the left.

Stepping up again, he pulled back his putter and heard the soft thunk as his club met the ball. It had eyes. He knew it did. Then the damn thing skirted the hole to the right and rolled a good five feet downhill.

"Shit," he heard Ben declare.

In the waning daylight it took two more putts to finish. Wordlessly, he picked up his ball and trudged toward the cart.

"Golf is a cruel game." Ben tried to commiserate. "A cruel, cruel game."

And so is business, Dirk thought as he loaded his clubs into Ben's SUV and blew on his hands to warm them. So is business.

2008

Dirk

June

"I'm gettin' too old for this, Dirk-honey." His mother blotted her forehead with her sleeve. "I swear to God that bakin' pies is a whole lot easier than deadheadin' all these petunias. You want this next row done, too?"

"Sure, Mom. Thanks." He continued to focus on the sea of yellow coreopsis he was trimming as he battled the vague guilt that gnawed at him from accepting her offer to help, then stopped long enough to tug open two of the heavy greenhouse doors. Immediately, the rush of early June morning air relieved the blanket of lethargy that had wrapped itself around him in the humid greenhouse.

"The boys've promised to come tomorrow so we'll be ready to start the summer sale on Monday. We've gotta move some of this stuff," he assured her.

"And?" Pausing from her rhythmic pinching to fix her gaze on him, his mom left her question hanging unanswered in the air.

"Nora said she'll help out right after the Fourth. She's

got her hands full lining up Obama reps for all the parades around here. She won't be in Rockwell that day, but the boys and I still hope to get to your place for the picnic."

"Hmm." His mother surveyed the purple row, rounded the corner and began attacking a mound of pink blossoms. "How about that other one?"

"Gina should be here in a little bit." His heart quickened as he wondered what colors his right-hand helper would throw together for an outfit today. She wasn't due for another hour, and already he found himself anticipating the sound of her throaty voice and the predictable pop of her gum.

"I'll work till she gets here." Grumbling under her breath, his mom whipped off her gloves and headed for the door. "These rubber things're makin' my hands sweat. I'm goin' out to the little house to get a pair of them cotton ones."

Shoot, he thought, she's so smart she'll probably figure out I've been staying out there most of the time. He hadn't wanted her to know how bad things had gotten between Nora and him and that he'd been crashing on the lumpy futon there for the last few nights rather than endure another confrontation with his wife in front of their sons.

Still, he was grateful that his mom was gone for a few moments. Now he could allow himself the luxury of letting his shoulders sag as he replayed the scene from two days ago when Ben had stopped in. His buddy had looked like he was going to a funeral.

"The bank's coming down hard on us and our customers." Ben's suit had seemed a couple of sizes too big for him as he'd stood there in the cluttered greenhouse office and delivered the news. "The guys on the loan committee in Chicago have told me you've gotta have twenty thousand dollars to them by August 1 or they'll repossess."

Dirk had lowered himself into the chair behind his desk. Trying to breathe calmly, he'd almost been felled by the smothering odor of fertilizers that consumed the heavy hot-house air. He'd motioned for Ben to have a seat on a nearby stool.

"I—I don't know how–" he'd stammered. He'd never seen Ben so pale and decided the smell must be bothering him too when he saw his buddy blink to clear his watering eyes.

Both discussed all the bad things that had happened and agreed that Dirk had overextended when he'd put on the ad-dition and invested in all that pond equipment. He'd really been crippled when three of his best commercial customers had decided to cut costs by buying all their plantings from the big box stores in Danville after he'd already stocked ev-erything he figured they'd want.

"So much for loyalty." Although his words were barely audible, he'd known Ben had understood his reference to the changing economic climate. When they'd exchanged limp handshakes, Dirk promised to do his best to round up some cash. Neither had said a word about golf.

Now he leaned against a counter overrun with rows of leggy petunias and lopsided marigolds. The blossoms that had brought such hope in the spring seemed to mirror his discouragement as they dangled from their planters.

He hated this feeling of being boxed in, pressured by the bank to pay, pressured by Nora to be a better dad, pressured even by himself to make a success of his dream business.

It reminded him of when he was a boy walking home from school and three bigger guys in his class surrounded him, threatening to beat him up because he was so little.

"Runt! Baby Runt!" they'd chanted as they came closer and took pokes at him. His face and body had stung from their jabs when he tried to defend himself. He'd smelled the rotten-toothed breath of Chauncey Gatlin as the bully drew back a fist to smash his nose. That was the moment his take-charge sister, Darcy, had grabbed Chauncey's hand in mid-air and yelled, "Hey, that's my brother! Leave him alone or I'll send Denny down here to whip your ass."

Darcy had settled it, just as efficiently as she handled any mouthy customers today at The Boulder. Chauncey and his cronies had slunk away. Dirk had wanted to taunt them, to yell that a girl had scared them off, but he knew he'd better leave well enough alone. Darcy'd helped him pick up his books, and later that night his other sister, Debbie, had made him a butterscotch sundae.

He sighed as he saw his mom returning with the cotton gloves. In other years, when he'd been under stress for one thing or another, he'd poured his energy into his own garden. But not this year. Only a few volunteer plants and a ton of weeds had sprouted in his back yard, and Nora's corners stood barren of any flowers.

"Sure smells musty out there. I opened some windows to let in some fresh air."

As Dirk continued snipping back dead geranium blossoms, he realized his mom hadn't stopped at the petunia section.

"You been stayin' out there?" She began to pluck at the geraniums as she spoke.

"What makes you think something like that?" He didn't look up. His mom had always been able to spot a lie from the expression in his eyes.

"It's all neat and tidy—like you always kept your stuff at home. The little house didn't used to be like that." She scrutinized him for a moment, then engulfed him in a hug.

"Oh, Dirk-honey, I don't know what's going on with you, but—" Drawing back sharply, she fixed her gray eyes on him. "You <u>have</u>. You <u>have</u> been stayin' out there. I can smell it in your clothes."

"I've been putting in such long hours out here." He still avoided her gaze.

"Long hours, my foot! You and Nora got troubles. Anybody with half a brain can see that." She returned to the geraniums, snapping off dried blooms with a vengeance. "And you got two boys that are startin' to run wild."

He continued working silently.

"Look at me, Dirk-honey. And listen to me. Listen to me real good."

When his eyes met hers, he saw the old fire in them, the resolve that had always kept her children in line. He squirmed, wishing Gina would burst through the door and get him off the hook.

"Now, I've been through all this. Oh my God, I've been through it all—shaky business, bad marriage, you name it. <u>I</u> left Bill, and that was the thing to do. For me. For all of us."

"Mom, it'll be—"

"Don't stop me. You get ahold of Nora and you work this thing out."

He didn't dare tell her he wasn't sure he wanted to work it

out. They'd run their course. She was immersed in the campaign, and, if he was truthful with himself, knew he couldn't wait to see Gina every day.

"You got them boys to consider," she continued. "They've just about been livin' over at Dougie's. Maria's been feedin' 'em and doin' their laundry. Cherisse worships the ground they walk on."

He clenched his clippers so hard they jumped from his hand and landed on the floor. He'd had no idea his kids had been spending so much time at his brother's. Hanging his head, he glanced at his mother.

"I mean it, Dirk-honey. You and Nora get your shit together. For the sake of the boys." Her eyes filled with tears. "And maybe mine, too. You know I've always loved Nora and I couldn't bear it—"

"Hey, everybody, I'm here!"

A splash of fuchsia breezed through the doorway as Gina made her grand entrance. Thank God, he thought. Maybe she'll come in and tell Mom she's trying to get us a booth at the Farmers' Market in Danville. And maybe later she and I will share a pizza out at the little house. And maybe . . .

Peeling off her gloves, his mom sighed. "I was just leavin'." As she passed him on her way to the side doors, she poked him in the ribs. "You remember what I told you. You hear?"

He did his best to push his mother's comments into the farthest corners of his mind so that he could don the daring-young-dude demeanor that he liked to wear when Gina was around.

"You sure know how to brighten up a place." He let his gaze wander over the hot pink t-shirt that looked like it was painted on and the lime green shorts that—well, he had to admit he loved the way they cupped her cute little butt. For a moment he allowed himself to wonder how it would feel if he could get her alone and peel off those shorts. Realizing the color of his face must match the shade of her shirt, he turned away and busied himself with the geraniums.

"You're gonna like this." Pop! "That guy I told you about says we can share his space at the Farmers' Market right after the Fourth. I say we go for it."

He felt his spirits soar. If they could get rid of a bunch of plants and break even on the pond equipment at his annual sale, he might be able to scrape together enough to keep those bank wolves away from his door. He attacked the geraniums with new enthusiasm.

Except for the rhythmic crackling of her gum, they worked silently and efficiently. Occasionally, he stopped to soak in the riot of color around him—the brave array of flowering plants that begged to be adopted and Gina's dazzling presence that he hoped would be a permanent fixture. She paused and shot a question in his direction.

"You going to the county fair in Danville next week?" He marveled at how she never missed a beat, snapping her gum, pinching off dead blossoms, making conversation at the same time.

"Don't know," he answered, hedging his bets.

"I've gotta go two nights. My niece is in the Little Miss

Vermilion County pageant on Tuesday, and my brother-in-law's in the tractor pull on Thursday. I won't be able to work late those days."

He paused briefly to consider that she had issued a statement of fact, not a request to take time off.

"I love the fair!" she emoted, moving from the display of pink snapdragons to yellow. "I can't wait to get me a coupla elephant ears and ride the tilt-a-whirl. You like the tilt-a-whirl?"

Shoot, the very idea of it made him want to puke.

"It's not my favorite," he admitted, amazed by the way the sun broke through the greenhouse panels to highlight the bluish sheen in her black hair.

"You'd better stay home then." Pop! "Maybe you're more of a merry-go-round kind of guy."

Literally saved by the tinkling of the bell in his office, he threaded his way through the tables of plants and into the office to wait on an elderly lady who wanted some "sturdy flowers" for her sister's grave.

He selected six of his strongest geraniums and a dozen marigolds.

"These should get you through the summer and into fall," he assured her. "The crew at the cemetery's pretty cool about watering everything if we get a dry spell."

Watching the lady's gnarled fingers struggle with the pennies as she counted out the exact change, he wondered if his mom might know who she was.

"Oh! That's wonderful!" Her smile was as warm as the June afternoon. "I'm from Ohio and don't get back to Rockwell very often." She dropped the coin purse into her canvas tote.

The little transaction made him feel good. At this point, he thought, <u>any</u> sale made him feel good. As he loaded her purchases into the trunk of her car, two other customers pulled up. Twenty minutes later they had relieved him of four more flats of annuals. Whistling an old Uncle Tommy tune, he kicked a stone as he made his way across the parking lot. At some time while he'd been peddling his plants, the gentle breeze had settled itself, leaving a heaviness in the air that felt more like August. He checked the haze in the western sky and wondered if it was hiding a late afternoon thunderstorm.

Back in the greenhouse, he found Gina scrutinizing the racks of seeds.

"We need to mark these down, you know. Nobody's going to buy them now at full price."

"I kinda thought I'd wait till after the Fourth." He hated to give away everything.

Her shrug transmitted the message, "Whatever." He made a mental note to put a twenty-per-cent off sign on each rack.

"What do you want done with all these tomato and pepper plants?" She poked among the trays of tall vegetable seedlings overdue to be tucked into a real garden. "I'm not sure—"

"Let me show you." He welcomed an excuse to sidle up next to her. Enjoying his height advantage, he reached for a plant and allowed the softness of her arm to brush his.

"Just trim 'em up a bit so they'll still put some of their strength in their roots." Bending over her, he could smell the inviting herbal aroma of her shampoo. When they were together later, he hoped he could bury his face in that sexy mop of hair.

Pop! She grinned and nodded.

As she calmly worked her way through the vegetable plants, he poured his own frenetic energy into rearranging the display of fountains for the upcoming sale. Bewildered by the storm of conflicting emotions that pummeled him, he marveled at the contentment he derived from Gina's presence while fighting off his mounting financial fears. The threat of losing Redbud Hill drove a nail into his stomach, reminding him of the time he'd guzzled too many Dr. Peppers in one afternoon when he was twelve.

He decided to chase away his negative thoughts by imagining the time he had planned with Gina after work. They'd freshen up a bit, run up to Barley's and pick up a pizza, then return to the little house. Maybe they'd grab some ice cream to have later. It was the "later" that was really playing mind games with him. He pictured a quiet evening with some of Uncle Tommy's provocative piano standards providing a velvety backdrop while he made his move.

By late afternoon, when soft rolls of thunder rumbled in the distance, he suggested that Gina freshen up in the little house while he washed and put on the clean set of clothes he kept in his office. Tossing on an extra splash of Brut, he locked up the greenhouse, and strode across the parking lot to find Gina. When she opened the door, he was dazzled by the orange-gold/canary print of her blouse tucked neatly into white shorts. Fiddling with a large gold hoop earring, she asked casually, "Could you hook my necklace for me? I can't get it myself."

Once again he felt over six feet tall as he stood behind her and nervously fumbled with the fastener. Inching toward her moussed black curls, he knew he could wait no longer. But the moment she heard the secure snap of the clasp, she stepped away and whirled around.

"Did I tell you I've got a part-time job in Danville this fall?" Her eyes twinkled like those of a child who'd just sneaked a cookie from her mom's jar. "The Steak 'n Shake near the college needs extra waitresses and I–"

"You–you won't be here in the fall?" His face stung as he tried to remain calm.

"Not to worry. I'll be back in the spring." Pop! "When you really need me." She lifted her chin confidently to convey the message that all would be well.

The ever-present knife in his stomach turned slowly.

"You're sure?" Realizing the musty smell of the little house was beginning to overpower her cologne, he put his hand on the futon to steady himself as his whole world crumbled around the edges.

"You bet! C'mon. Let's go get that pizza. I'm starved."

Although he felt as if her news had aged him ten years, Gina seemed energized by her change of clothes and the prospect of her favorite pizza. As they drove to Barley's, she chattered on about the fair, the Farmers' Market, and her new job.

The spicy smell of pizza sauce and yeasty aroma of Barley's own dough greeted him as he opened the door for Gina.

"Hey," she purred.

Dirk tried to ignore her one syllable, dipped in honey and rounded off warmly, that she'd directed at the guy who'd made their pizza.

"Hey, yourself." Barley whistled under his breath. His little fox eyes gleamed as he absorbed her image in one sweeping glance. Turning his attention to Dirk, he asked, "Hungry tonight, my friend?"

"You bet." He felt peppered by needles of uncertainty. Clumsily, he sorted through his coins, feeling he must look like the old lady who'd bought flowers from him that afternoon. "Thanks, Barley. See you later."

"Yeah," Barley drawled, never taking his eyes off Gina. "See you. Later."

As he placed a protective arm around Gina's back to steer her toward the parking lot, Dirk caught a glimpse of Barley's hungry gaze. Shuddering, he guided her to his truck as quarter-sized raindrops pelted the cardboard box that held their supper.

Back at the nursery, they laughed as they ran through the downpour. Awkwardly, Dirk handed the box to Gina so he could jiggle the key in the lock. When he opened the door, he realized his mom was right. The little house did smell like mildew. He'd invest in a strong deodorizer first thing in the morning.

He pulled out a couple of Uncle Tommy's best CDs, fished out two icy Miller Lites from the fridge, and handed Gina a paper plate. She opened the soggy box and scooped two large slices onto her plate right next to her wad of gum. He debated on three slices but settled on two for starters.

Perched on opposite ends of the futon, they exchanged

appreciative murmurs as they attacked their pizza and swigged their beer. Dirk closed his eyes for a moment and let the sensations of the zesty pizza and icy beer merge with the buttery sounds of "This Time the Dream's on Me" emanating from Uncle Tommy's piano.

"I'll get seconds," he announced, then dropped another slice onto Gina's plate. When he'd taken one for himself, he returned to the futon. This time he casually settled himself on the middle pillow, close enough so their arms could touch.

"You've got sauce on the end of your nose." Tenderly he dabbed her face with a napkin. The rain drummed on the metal roof, providing a rhythmic accompaniment to the opening chords of Uncle Tommy's lazy rendition of "How High The Moon."

"In fact," he continued, "you've got the cutest nose."

Shoot, he thought, what a lame line! Impulsively he shed his regrets and touched the tip of her nose with his lips. He sighed, then pulled her closer and gave her the kiss he'd been dreaming about ever since the first day she'd walked into his greenhouse. The lingering mint from her gum was sweet, inviting.

Shocked, she jumped up and headed for the fridge.

"What the hell? You sure know how to surprise a girl!" Pulling out two beers, she handed him one and planted herself on the wooden chair across the room.

"You've been surprising me for a long time." He patted the seat next to him. "I thought we should finally take it to the next level."

Rattled, she took frantic little sips of her beer. Neither spoke. Finally, she cleared her throat.

"But Dirk, I've–I've never–never led you on." She

162

pushed her hair back from her face. "I–I've never given you any—well, you know, signals. Do I have to spell it out for you? N-E-V-E-R. Never!"

He watched as she turned ashen beneath her makeup.

"Oh, Gina, you're a walking signal. Everywhere you go!" He eyed her over the top of his beer can. "If Nora had a fraction of your sexy energy, we'd have ten kids by now." Mentally he kicked himself for introducing his wife's name into his long-awaited seduction scene.

She sighed, placed her beer on the table, and rejoined him on the futon.

"Now look at me." Her tone sounded just like his mom's. "You and Nora are a good pair. You're just—well, running off in different directions right now." Her breath was still coming in little spurts.

He laughed mirthlessly. "You got that right."

"But you and me? No way!" She took his face in her hands. "Look at me. I'm a fun-type girl. I like my good times. But I don't go for guys who like music—well, like this." She waved her hand toward the CD player.

"I want my songs to rock. And I want a guy who lives on the edge." Her dark eyes were serious. "No offense, but that ain't you, honey. That ain't you. Good God Gertrude! You're married!"

The word "married" carved new paths of pain through his gut. Rubbing his stomach, he saw the determination in her face and felt his expectations ooze out of him like a leaky tire.

"I sure don't feel married." He shook his head. "Where're you going?"

She picked up her gold purse, stripped open a new stick

of gum, and dropped it into her mouth. "Somewhere." Her words were muffled by the wad she was corralling.

When her gaze averted his, he knew—knew exactly where .

"You're going to Barley's." He couldn't believe he'd called her bluff. But there it was, out in the open. Somehow, he'd sensed it earlier when they'd picked up their order. "And not for pizza."

"No. Not for pizza." She studied him for a moment, then dug to the bottom of her purse for her keys. "I'll see what kind of games he's running in his back room tonight, just like I've been doing for a long time. And then?" Pop! Pop! "You never know."

"God." He sat on the futon with his head in his hands.

"I'll still work for you the rest of the summer. If you want me. We've gotta get ready for the Farmers' Market." Her throaty tones emphasized every word. "Just no more of this funny stuff. Got it?"

Nodding, he felt himself unravel inside. He could hear the defiant punctuation of her gum and smell the rain as she let herself out.

Alone inside, he cringed, just as he had years ago when Chauncey Gatlin was closing in on him. He'd just been humiliated by the hottest girl between here and Danville. And the bankers from Chicago were hovering around the corner, licking their chops to get their hands on his business.

As Uncle Tommy's mournful rendition of "Cry Me a River" filled the dank room, he wondered how much lower he could sink.

Doug

Mid-July

"No problem, Deb." Doug tried to remain calm as he slammed down the phone. Hell, planning this boat trip was the worst one yet! David had canceled his annual visit back to Rockwell because of a work project, Darcy had a big wedding to cater, and now Debbie'd told him she and Kirk were taking off for a week in New England. Even Cherisse was going on a sleepover on Saturday night.

"What's the matter, kochany?" Maria called from their living room, where she was stenciling designs on one wall. He could hear the ladder squeak as she made her way down the steps

"Hell, nobody can come." Reaching into the cookie jar, he retrieved two of her plump Polish sugar cookies to console himself. His heart flipped as it always did when he saw her with her hair tied back and paint-speckled cheeks.

She poured a cup of coffee, plucked out a cookie and sat down on one of their bright green kitchen chairs.

"So who've we got so far?" She bit into the cookie and

uttered an "Umm."

"Just you and me." He warmed up his own coffee. "And Mom. If you can believe that. Who'd ever thought she would want to go again?"

"She had a great time last year. In spite of her fears." Studying him over the top of her mug, she was silent for a moment then asked, "How about the boys? If Dirk and Nora could go too, it'd be a good family outing for all of them."

Dirk? Damn, he realized as his face grew warm, he hadn't even thought about his youngest brother! Dirk had been so distracted lately that he was content to let his sons grab their meals and hang out with Doug and Maria. "I'll run out to the greenhouse and see."

But as the tires of his Grand Prix crunched their way past the cheery sign for Redbud Hill, he sensed a pervasive atmosphere of gloom. Hell, he thought as he strolled through the greenhouse door, the whole place feels forlorn.

"Hey, bro!" He was determined to start his conversation on an upbeat note. "I'm looking for some late summer flowers for Maria. Got anything?"

Dirk waved a limp arm in the direction of his straggly plants.

"Lots of stuff." He shrugged. "But probably nothing she'd really want."

"Well, gimme a flat of them whatcha-ma-call-its—those yellow and orange things." Man, he didn't even need these damn plants. He just had to snag the interest of his mopey brother.

"The marigolds? You got 'em." Dirk seemed to spring to life as he scanned his collection of droopy flowers and picked out the healthiest bunch.

Doug pulled a few bills from his wallet and handed them to his brother. "What're you all doing this weekend?" he asked casually. "We're taking an overnight trip on the boat and thought you all might want to join us."

"Well, first off, forget Nora. She'll be in Danville. The campaign, you know. Or whatever." Dirk's smile was tight, his tone bitter. "And I've gotta stay here and work. Gina'll be in and out." He paused, suddenly hopeful. "But Carter and Logan? I bet they'd love it."

Doug swallowed. He guessed he and Maria could handle the boys for the whole weekend. And if the guys gave them trouble, there was always Mom who'd make them behave.

"Sure. Why not?"

"This'll be the highlight of their summer." Dirk seemed full of gratitude as he filed Doug's bills in the cash register. "And thanks for the business."

"No problem." Doug picked up the flat of pungent marigolds, then set them down again. The damn things made his nose tickle. As he hauled them to his car, he wondered at the success of his mission. Not only had he gained a bunch of half-dead flowers he didn't really want, but he'd also acquired a couple of boys for the whole weekend! Maybe a cold beer at Nick's would soothe his nerves. He gave Maria a quick call from his cell, then parked his car in Rigoni's lot.

It took a moment for his eyes to adjust to the dim light. Ambling across the room to the bar, he inhaled and felt better already. Funny, he thought, how the sour smell of a good ale in a dark room on a sunny day could raise your spirits.

"Sox winning?" he asked as he settled himself on a stool

near the middle of the bar.

"You gotta be joking." Nick poured him a draft. "What's up?

Between swigs of the foamy brew, he unloaded his complaints, confessing he was tired of trying to make everyone happy with weekend trips.

"Ah, the joys of boat ownership." Nick toweled out some mugs and put them back on the shelf. "Never heard you complaining when you were riding in mine."

Doug let the comment slide and continued his tale of woe.

"It's just so damn hard to get the family together. Even for a weekend of fun." He put down his mug and studied Nick. "Why don't you come?" he asked. "The boys can bunk together, and there'd be room for both you and Amy."

"Not a chance. But thanks. We've gotta go to a big wedding. Amy's bought a new dress and everything." Nick shook his head. "Can't get out of that one."

"Oh, yeah—probably the one that Darcy's catering." Doug sighed.

"Why don't you ask <u>him</u>?" Nick spoke a little too loudly as he pointed his thumb toward the end of the bar.

In the soft light, Doug realized for the first time that Denny was seated on the last stool. He shot Nick a fierce glare that his buddy ignored.

"Hi, Grumpy." His oldest brother let a lazy smile spread across his face as he picked up his beer and eased onto the seat next to Doug. "Go where?"

"He's got one spot to fill on a weekend cruise up on Lake Michigan," Nick flashed a mischievous grin at Doug. "You oughtta join him."

"I'm all ears." Denny's voice was low. "Never been on your boat before. Maybe it's about time, huh?"

"Sure. Uh, sure." Doug secretly thought, "Shit!" as he squinted his eyes at Nick with the message that warned he'd get him for this. "Yeah, sure."

"Who's goin'?" Denny sure resembled their dad, Doug thought. They shared that same knack for putting you on the spot while verbally walking all over you.

"Just some of the family—Me, Maria, Carter, Logan." He stopped right there. No use mentioning Mom at this point. Denny'd only let loose with a tirade about how their mother had mistreated their dad when she left him.

"Not Runt?" Denny raised an eyebrow and motioned for another beer.

"Nope. Gotta run his business," he explained.

"Sounds like it's runnin' him. From what I hear." Denny took a penny from his pocket. "Let's see what I'll do this weekend. Heads, I go. Tails, I don't." Flipping it onto the bar, he watched as the coin spun and settled. "Heads," he observed. "Guess I'll be goin' with you. Thanks for the invite."

Doug could feel himself blanch as he worked out the details with Denny for the following Saturday. When Denny said he'd meet them at the marina, Doug gave him directions and tried to ignore the big ball of dread that was already building inside him.

"You're such a pushover," Maria scolded after he pulled into their driveway with the flat of tired marigolds and the news that Denny would be joining them. She glanced up from cleaning her paint brushes on their outdoor work table.

"Did you tell him your mom was going?"

"Not yet," he mumbled. "Might be best if <u>she</u> doesn't know either. Then they'll get there and find out they're stuck with each other. We might have us a high old time!"

"You never know." Maria dumped the turpentine behind a bush. "You just never know. Now, where am I going to plant these marigolds?"

Doris

Mid-July

*H*ey, Everyone, it's me again. Just checking in and letting off steam as usual. Ha Ha!

You guys wont believe this but I'm going out with Dougie this weekend for another boat ride and I'm not even scared. Well maybe a little.

He's getting some of the family together, I'm not sure who all is going, but I'll bring some food and we'll have some fun. I hope. We're going to stay all night on the boat this time. I wish it was just Dougie driving us four girls so we could sleep over the way we used to do in seventh grade. That would have to be one of our best days ever.

Remember how we used to play that game? Best and worst days of our lives? Im starting to feel like Im having a worst day everytime I see Dirk. He's just got his life all screwed up. Him and Nora don't pay attention to their boys or each other, so he keeps checking out that floozy Gina that works for him. I just hope he wont do something stupid. You

171

know what I mean.

His business that started out so good is drying up. I know he's scared he's gonna lose it and he's scared to talk about it. Dont tell anyone but sometimes at nite I cant sleep for worrying about him. If you all was here I could talk about it with you. But your not.

Its starting to feel like forever since we were all together. Seems like stuff just keeps popping up that keeps us apart. I wish we all couldve went to Rosie's last summer. Me & her had a nice lunch but we missed you Cheryl and Kate.

Cheryl, there wont be nuthing this Oct. that will keep us from coming to your new apartment. I know you were busy last fall with your hospital board but you clear your calendar this year, you hear?

Kate, we hope things have settled down for you and Marty. It had to be terrible hard to move from your nice house into that assisted living place last fall but I bet its a relief to have help with Marty when you need it. You can have a day off and take the train into Chicago for our big lunch. Maybe we should have baloney sandwiches for old times sake. Ha Ha!

Rosie, we know your going to be in Chicago anyway to see Colton's new baby. When is it due? If its a girl, are they going to name it Rosie? Ha Ha! Are him and his girlfriend going to get married or what?

I never thought I'd say this, but I wish Dirk could be having as much fun with Alan's money as Dougie is. You know what I mean. I'll let you know all about my big boat ride. Maybe next summer I can get Dougie to take the

*four of us out for a slumber party. Now wouldn't that be
something?*

    Best friends forever–Doris

Doug

Late July

"Thanks."

Doug heard Denny's curt response and saw him avoid their mother's scrutiny as he accepted the scoopful of homemade potato salad she dropped onto his plastic plate.

"Damn," he whispered to Maria, "This was <u>not</u> such a good idea." Deftly, he split a large wave with the bow to avoid being rocked excessively.

In the roar as the wave rushed against the boat, Maria winked at Carter and Logan to let them know that rough seas were great fun. "Keep smiling, kochany," she murmured. "We've survived an entire afternoon together, and it's bound to get better."

Squinting into the early evening sun, he knew he could only hope. That morning the five of them had swapped jokes and old stories during their drive from Rockwell to the marina. He'd welcomed the beckoning smell of open water when he'd begun to load their supplies onto the "Windfall" and chuckled to himself when he'd seen his mom showing

Carter and Logan around the boat like she owned the thing. After an unseasonably cool week, he'd been glad to feel the warmth of the sun on the back of his neck as he checked the boat. The weekend was shaping up to be a good one after all. Well, it had been, he recalled, until his brother had shown up.

"Got room for one more?" He'd glanced up and seen Denny munching on his trademark toothpick and moseying down the pier. "Hey, Grumpy—pretty nice hunka junk you've got here."

Trying to pass himself off as a laid-back seaman, Denny had caught his foot when he'd tried to board, stumbled over a seat, and managed to land with a thud on both feet inside the boat.

"What the–?"

Doug had held his breath when his mom, startled by the commotion, emerged from the cabin. First, she'd stared at Denny in disbelief, then at Doug as if he'd betrayed her. "What the hell?" she'd finished weakly.

"Hi, Mom." Denny'd shifted his toothpick from one cheek to the other. "Nice day for a ride. Hi guys, Maria." He'd greeted the rest with a mock salute.

"Hey, Denny." Doug had been relieved to hear Maria save the moment. "Beer's in the cooler over there. Carter, Logan—come help me show your Uncle Denny around. Mom, would you mind getting out those plastic glasses?"

Doug would never forget the way his mother had stiffened–like a wary animal who'd been trapped.

"Don't do nuthin' extra on my account." Denny'd ogled Maria with the leer that he gave every girl he met. "I drink mine straight from the can. Just like my dad." His narrowed eyes, zeroing in on their mom, had emphasized his message.

So, Doug had realized as he settled into to the captain's seat, the mood is set. This is going to be a helluva long week-end. Damn that Nick for putting me in a position where I had to ask Denny! Damn it to hell that my mother and my brother can't get along for once. Damn it that I ever bought this thing in the first place. I could be out enjoying myself on Nick's boat, just cruising around Lake Vermilion without a care in the world. Or home cleaning my garage. Damn.

"We're gonna head up along the skyline, have supper and watch the sunset," he'd explained to his family before he started the engine. "We'll come back here to dock for the night and tomorrow we'll take a look at the Indiana shore before we close 'er up and head home.

"You guys all take turns sitting up here with me." He'd patted the plump white cushion across from him. "We'll start with the youngest. Okay, Logan? You can help me take it out of the bay."

Glancing up at the bow, he'd watched Maria laughing as she identified landmarks in the bay to Carter as they cruised toward the big lake. Denny'd craned his neck to take in all he could, waving to passing boats as if the "Windfall" were his. Their mom, riveted to her seat, had stared straight ahead.

"Grand-do and Uncle Denny don't get along too good, do they?" Logan had stated the obvious.

"You got that right, dude." He'd looked over at his neph-ew and grinned. "But we're workin' on it. See those build-ings over there? That's Chicago. Let's go check out the city, then it's your turn to drive."

Now, with their bellies full and an approaching sunset

that promised to be postcard-worthy, he was ready to give the wheel to Denny. At least that'd put some space between his mom and his brother. Damn, he wondered sometimes if his own family was more dysfunctional than Pete Nolan's.

Doris

The Same Evening

"I sure hope that da—darn fool knows what he's doing." Doris braced herself against the seat and barricaded the cards so they wouldn't slide off the cabin table. She and Logan had become bored with waiting for the sunset and had dealt out a hand of double solitaire.

"You and Uncle Denny don't like each other very much, do you, Grand-do?" Logan laid down a run of spades on the three that she'd put out for play. "He sure did like your coconut cake though."

She glanced up and saw the questioning look in the gray eyes that mirrored her own.

"Wait'll he sees the apple pie that's in the cooler for tomorrow," she answered, trying to skirt questions about her relationship with her oldest son. "Shi—shoot! You're too fast for me." It rankled her to think that her grandson had gotten her distracted and now she'd missed a play on the seven of diamonds.

"But you two talk funny to each other. When you do

talk," he persisted. "Not like the way you talk to my dad and Uncle Doug."

"It's complicated. It goes back a long way." Triumphantly, she plunked down a seven and eight of clubs. "I guess maybe your Uncle Denny reminds me too much of his dad."

Logan scanned the board and was able to play a nine on the pile of clubs.

"You didn't like him either, did you? I mean, Dad says you got divorced." He put down his hand. "I'm stuck. But you guys had six kids."

"Oh yeah, Logan, we had six kids all right. But he was mean." She surveyed the cards and admitted she had no more plays. "Oh, he never hit me, but he did hurt me. Hurt me bad. With his words."

Logan's eyes grew wide. "Was he a bully?"

"Yeah, honey, I guess he was. A big-time bully. And a lot of other things." Even today, after all those years, she could feel the searing pain of Bill's hateful words that had made her believe she was a worthless piece of shit. "Let's play another game." Quickly, she dealt out her deck and waited for him to do the same.

Logan, instead, was thoughtful.

"But Uncle Denny doesn't seem like a bully." He struggled to make sense of the situation.

"I'm not sure he is," she conceded.

"He talks big. He likes to brag, but you know what's weird, Grand-do?" Still holding his deck of cards, he searched her face. "Sometimes, to me anyway, he seems lonesome. Like he feels he's missing out on something."

"Well, it's his own da—darn fault," she barked. "You

watch. And you'll see. Now, c'mon, let's play cards. We're gonna fix s'mores after the sun goes down."

She loved the way Logan brightened. But she had to fight to control her hand from shaking as she played the next game. Logan's comments had let loose a whole bunch of butterflies in her stomach. She recalled that first summer with Bill and how much she'd loved him when she was fifteen and how proud she'd been of Denny, her firstborn, when he was a child. If Denny was missing out on something, as her grandson had suggested, so was she. Oh my God, so was she! How could it have all gone so wrong?

Doug

Some of their tension, he felt, seemed to be evaporating as brilliant pink streaks from the sunset faded into soft puffs behind the clump of suburban buildings. All the guys on board had wanted "one more time" at the wheel, and, with Denny driving full speed ahead, they'd cruised a little farther north than he'd ever ventured before. Maria had opened the electric grill they'd had bolted to a rail so they could cook their hot dogs in the open air. She liked to refer to it as their "pretend campfire."

"Makes the 'Windfall' seem cozier," she explained,

"We're really going to sleep on this, aren't we?" For the first time since they'd left the marina, Carter seemed to comprehend that the "Windfall" would be his home away from home for the night. "In those bedrooms underneath?"

"It'll be like bunking at our house—only with a little rocking. You'll sleep like a baby." Maria tossed Carter a bag of marshmallows. "Here. Open these. We've got some long sticks for toasting. At least we're going to try!"

Doug could feel the untouched topic of Dirk and his

problems hovering over them like a threatening cloud. Still, nobody brought up the subject until Logan broke the long silence.

"Too bad Dad couldn't have come along." He stuck a marshmallow on a long fork and licked his fingers. "I think he mighta liked this."

"Yeah. But then there wouldn't have been room for <u>me</u>," Denny chortled, but Doug thought he saw a hint of regret in his brother's eyes. "Your timing was pretty good for a change, Grumpy. I just cut that little field of wheat and the beans and corn're still doin' their thing. Yep—pretty good." He slapped together a gooey s'more and wolfed it down in two bites.

"Harvesting sure can be a tricky time," their mom mused. "Like playing Russian roulette with the weather."

Denny looked up and studied their mom. "You remember?"

"Of course–like it was yesterday! Some things you never forget." Everyone fell silent as their mom spoke. "Me—well, me 'n your dad turned out some decent crops in our day." She cleared her throat. "Well, you know—early on. When you was too little to remember."

"But I do," he challenged, warming another marshmallow to soft, tan perfection.

"Do what?"

Doug thought his mom looked at Denny like she was seeing him for the first time in years.

"Remember." Denny's face flushed with his old cockiness. "I remember riding the tractor with you while David took his nap and Debbie was in her baby swing under that big old oak tree."

"No way!" Doris retorted. "You're shittin' me. Just like always."

Carter and Logan snickered.

"Grand-do!" Logan exclaimed in mock disgust.

"Keep it up, Uncle Denny," Carter urged. "We wanna hear this stuff, too."

Afraid to breathe, Doug gently guided the boat south back toward the city. The engine chugged in the background as his mom and oldest brother hashed over the tales that Denny had dredged up from his earliest memories.

He heard Denny recall the time his mom's friend, Kate, had visited and brought each one of them a book "when we were real little."

He felt the closeness of his brothers and sisters when Denny talked about all the kids piling into bed with her so she could read to them at bedtime.

He chuckled to himself when Denny mentioned their dad's touchy stomach and his outspoken opinions about food.

However, as Denny edged toward the subject of Bill Lochschmidt and his mean ways, he fell silent again. Doug wondered if he saw his mom and brother exchange furtive but softer glances.

"Are we getting farther out?" Carter broke the mood with his concern for their whereabouts. "Those lights from the shore seem dimmer."

"Could be a little bit of fog out there. I'm going to kick it up a notch and take her back to the marina."

Damn, he thought, I got too caught up in my own family

stories! Now it's darker than I'd like and Carter's right. That fog could give us some trouble. Increasing his speed, he peered into the cloud that seemed to be swallowing them. The thickening air felt damp on his cheeks, almost like mist from the lake. Beneath the pleasant murmuring of his family up on the bow, he could hear Carrie Underwood's "All American Girl" reverberating from their little radio in the cabin below.

"Me 'n Denny's goin' down to put this stuff away," his mom called.

"Sure thing," he yelled, trying not to let his concern show in his voice. Damn, this stuff was getting thicker by the minute! He jerked, startled by Maria's touch on his arm.

"Oh, kochany, it was so good to see your family like that." She snuggled against him. "You know, laughing over old times." Nestling into his sleeve, she sighed contentedly, then jumped. "Whoa. You think we should slow down? I can't even see the shore."

She wandered over to the side of the boat.

"I—I can barely see the boys! We've gotta get to a dock!" Her voice faded in the mist. "Carter! Logan! Come in here and get down in the cabin!"

"In a minute," Logan responded. "This is pretty cool."

"Now!" she directed in her best school-teacher form. When she heard nothing, she said, "I'm going out there to get them."

"Careful," he warned. "Could be slippery. We should be back in twenty minutes." He knew he was lying. Twenty minutes would get them halfway. Maybe. And he knew he was going too fast, but this whole thing was too damn eerie. He felt like he was steering a ghost ship through vapors in a sci-fi movie, searching for a mythical island.

He glanced at his instruments, but they didn't tell him a damn thing. He didn't have any idea where the hell he was! This was scarier than anything he'd ever done in his whole stupid life. His hoodie, soaked with fog and nervous sweat, clung to him like a piece of plastic wrap. Debating with himself about trying to drop anchor, and praying for the Lord's protection while they waited it out, he prepared to cut his speed when–BAM!

He held tight to the wheel. Damn it to hell! They'd hit something. Something really hard. Something that didn't give. Something that stood its ground. Amid screams from the boys and Maria, there were sounds of angry churning water below and the most sickening scrunching noise he'd ever heard. He stared in disbelief when his side of the boat cracked and begin to separate. Waves gushed through the hole, ripping the bow with their force. His stomach lurched as he realized he'd lost sight of everyone who'd been standing along the rail.

"Maria!" he shouted.

In what seemed like a lifetime, he stood paralyzed as the water chewed a jagged edge inches from the spot where he was rooted. His half, stripped of its balance, leaned to one side as it floundered and began to sink. Mortally wounded, the "Windfall" moaned, its sturdy man-made materials surrendering to nature's superior strength.

Stay calm, stay calm, he ordered himself frantically. Grasping the wheel, he yanked his cell from his pocket, hit 911, and yelled a garbled message, unsure whether anyone heard.

"Maria! Maria!"

He rode his chunk of the wreckage into the water. Damn, it was colder than hell. And darker, too, except for the whiteness of the fog. The damn fog. Carrie Underwood's snappy lyrics had been snuffed, replaced by the groaning of the "Windfall" as it agonized in the trauma.

"Over here! We're over here!" Through the soupiness he heard Maria call. Grabbing the remnant of a seat that floated beside him, he paddled in the direction of her voice.

"Got the boys. Hanging on," she shouted.

Through the murk, he forced his legs through the arctic water until he saw shadows appear in front of him Maria was hugging a piece of styrofoam with one hand and applying pressure to Carter's forehead with the other. Logan was clinging to a cushion with his right arm, while the left dangled at his side.

"Here—I'll take him." Carter felt like a feather when Maria transferred him. Doug pulled a wet glove from the pocket of his hoodie and held it tight against the spurting gash on the boy's face.

God, he thought, this is the part where I should wake up. Disoriented, he glanced around wildly, panicked that they were imprisoned by the dense gray cloud. Only the cracking sounds of the pieces of his prized boat as it lost its battle with the lake told him what he could not see.

"Gotta hang on!" He gulped and choked, trying not to inhale the rushing water. "The Coast Guard or somebody'll find us." He wished he could believe that. For the moment, at least, the four of them were okay.

Four of them? What the hell?

"Mom!" he screamed. "Mom! Denny!" His words faded into the fog.

There was no answer.

Doris

The Same Evening

In her wildest dreams she'd never imagined that in her lifetime she and Denny could hold a halfway sane conversation. About farming, of all things. On a boat, of all places! She couldn't wait to tell Rosie, Cheryl, and Kate. They wouldn't believe her.

She'd always thought s'mores were overrated—too many sweets all squished together, in her opinion. But she did like Hershey bars, so she indulged in six squares of milk chocolate. But she drew the line at marshmallows warmed on an electric grill. She preferred hers burned to a crisp, the way she'd always done at the wiener roasts back in eighth grade.

Tapping her foot to Carrie Underwood, she broke off two more chocolate squares and licked the stickiness from her lips. Denny hummed as he fixed himself one last s'more, while Carter and Logan debated whether a Quarter Pounder was better than a Big Mac. Maybe–just maybe–Dougie had known what he was doing when he bought the boat. She was considering this revelation when—BAM!

"What the–" It was all she had time to say. With the boat suddenly lurching wildly, she grabbed for something—anything–and singed her hand on the hot grill. As she let go, she lost her footing and fell to the rolling floor. The table holding their cooler wrenched itself from its fasteners and thudded onto her legs, pinning her to the floor. She bumped her head as she tried to fight her way out of a corner, and when she succeeded, she found herself thrashing in the waves. Debris bounced around her, assaulting her from all directions.

Still, it was the forceful gurgling that terrified her as the frigid water lapped her cheeks. Twisting from side to side, she tried to paddle. Then the pain hit, searing jagged bolts that raced up her legs. She couldn't move.

"I'm not gonna pass out," she vowed. "Not gonna pass out. Not gonna pass out."

She tried to yell for help, but no sound came from her throat.

"Dougie!" she mouthed. "Dougie!"

"Not gonna pass out, not gonna . . ."

Before the darkness carried her off, she felt arms under her, supporting her. God's, maybe?

"I've got you, Mom," were the last words she heard.

Dirk

Early the Next Morning

Stupid phone! Who'd be calling? He squinted at the clock on his bedside table. It showed three a.m.

"Yeah." His mind was still wrapped around his dream— that he'd been hired to furnish all the plantings for a huge new office complex in Rockwell (like that was going to happen) and his sons and Nora were cheerily digging holes in the soil to place the seedlings (like that was going to happen either). Inhaling deeply, he breathed in the rich aroma of the black soil.

"Yeah," he repeated, instinctively glancing at Nora's pillow and recalling that she'd stayed in Danville because of a late hog roast and early parade the next morning.

Instantly, his dream evaporated as he tried to make sense of Doug's words. Through intermittent static, his older brother shouted something about an accident. An accident with the boat.

His senses jangled into alertness, Dirk held his breath.

They'd all been taken to a hospital—Rush, in Chicago.

Doug's connection kept breaking up.

Dirk felt his midnight snack rising in his throat.

"The boys've been treated in the ER but wanna come home. We need you." Doug's voice was strained.

"I'll be there. Soon's I can." Feeling the phone sliding in his sweaty palm, Dirk tightened his hold on it.

"You know how to get here—Dan Ryan to the Taylor Street exit. Get off and go over to Ashland and follow the signs." His brother sounded worn, old, shaky.

"The boys're okay though?" He needed his brother's re-assurance as the reality of the message was beginning to sink in.

"Carter's got a big gash in his forehead that they're sew-ing up right now. Looks like–" Doug paused, "looks like Logan's got a broken arm, but they'll put it in a splint and he can go home."

"Everybody else?" His mind was trying to recall who all had been on this trip.

"Maria's being treated for shock and exposure." Doug's breath was shallow. "Me 'n Denny're pretty tuckered out." There was hesitation in his voice, still some undelivered message.

"Mom!" Dirk's mind cleared in an instant. "Where's Mom?"

"She's here. But—"

"But what?" A chill consumed him.

"She's pretty beat up. Hurt bad." Doug's voice quavered. Was he crying? "We–we almost lost her out there . . . I don't know . . ."

"I'm on my way."

Trembling, he dropped the phone on its dock, threw on some clothes, and was out the door. As his truck hurtled over back roads toward I-57, he realized he'd left home without a plan. He punched in Nora's number on his cell but was greeted with the "No Service" message. Shoot!

Goosing the gas pedal, he heard the gravel spin beneath him as he sped through the pre-dawn dark speckled with lingering tufts of fog. With only his thoughts and fears for companions, he turned up the ramp to the Interstate and raced toward the first lights of the city.

Doug

The Same Morning

Had the clock on the waiting room wall stopped? He studied his watch. Nope. 5:19 a.m. Rubbing his sore left elbow, he wondered how time could move so slowly in a hospital. Last time he'd checked, the thing had read 5:06— and that seemed like two hours ago.

Carter was propped up in a chair across from him, half-conscious and exhausted. A giant bandage spanned his forehead. Logan lay behind a curtain in one of those sterile cubicles waiting for a technician to put a splint on his arm. He'd have to have his mom or dad take him to an orthopedic guy in Danville in a couple of days to have it set.

He couldn't believe Denny was curled up in a love seat and sleeping like a baby in the middle of the ruckus that surrounded them. Doors swung open and doors swung shut, squeaking every time they moved. People darted in and out, shouting to one another like they were hopped up on bad drugs. And the smell. That damn hospital smell! He'd always prided himself on having a strong stomach, but that mix of disinfectant, blood, and God-only-knew-what-else made him feel pukey and lightheaded.

In one corner an old woman snored, her head thrown back, her toothless mouth wide open. In another corner a knot of Hispanic family members whimpered and prayed as they anticipated news from a doctor. He wondered what had brought them here.

He began to pace as he waited for permission to see Maria. He'd feel better when he could talk with her.

Then there was Mom. He broke into a sweat that dampened the hot pink Rush University Medical Center Hospital t-shirt the ER nurse had given him when he'd arrived with the ambulance blanket draped over his scraped and bleeding shoulders. The EMTs who'd picked them up had speculated she could have breaks in both legs and possible internal injuries. She'd been whisked away into the bowels of the hospital, and he'd had to be content with any crumbs of information the ER staff could feed him.

Brushing a tear from his cheek, he glanced at the clock again. 5:28. Damn! Where the hell <u>was</u> Dirk? How long could it take to get from Rockwell? Needing something, anything, to do, he thumbed through an old copy of *Field & Stream* and tossed it back on the table. He hadn't had a cigarette since he'd suffered through his divorce from Tonya, but he sure could use one now!

He'd already made his calls. Nora'd picked up her cell and said she'd be there. Swearing softly, she'd asked why Dirk hadn't notified her. Doug had replied that he didn't know.

Next, silly as it had seemed, he'd contacted David down

near Atlanta–woken him up from a sound sleep. But he'd been glad he called his older brother. Even at a distance, David had known what to do. He'd told Doug that his old Purdue buddy, a fellow named Thaddeus Strabowski, was on the orthopedic staff at Rush. David had said he'd call him right away and see that "Suds," as he referred to him, was on top of things.

Doug wasn't sure he trusted a guy called "Suds" with the health of his mom, but David had never given him bad advice. Not yet, anyway.

He'd decided to notify his sisters when he had more information. Debbie was in New England, and Darcy'd probably just gone to bed after catering that big wedding reception. He'd let Darcy tell Aunt Violet. He was running on empty himself right now and doubted he could deal with his addled, strong-willed aunt.

At 5:36, when the doors opened again, he hardly recognized Dirk. Uncombed, unshaven, his shirt buttoned wrong, he stumbled into the room, glanced at Doug, and headed straight for Carter. Minutes behind him came Nora, berating Dirk so loudly that even the snoring old woman sat bolt upright. The Hispanic family, jolted by Nora's vocabulary, huddled closer. Poor Carter sat like a forgotten lump, while Dirk tried to explain to Nora that there'd been no cell service when he'd tried to call her. Denny merely opened an eye, gave a small wave, and turned over.

Deciding he'd better play the role of the big brother, Doug shuffled over to them, placed his hands on Nora's shoulders, and announced he'd tell them exactly what had happened—as far as he knew.

"I don't think Carter feels much like talking right now. I'll get you a cup of coffee and fill you in." As he headed toward the snack bar, he glanced down. "Looks like you couldn't decide which pair to wear." He couldn't help but snicker. Dirk observed his mismatched shoes and shrugged.

After Doug handed them their coffee and pulled up a plastic chair, he sketched out the details as clearly as his muddled mind would allow.

A dense fog had hit fast. When he'd tried to hightail it back to the marina, he'd gotten confused and had driven inside the buoy markers. He'd hit something—maybe a jagged old metal pier–with such force that everyone had been thrown into the water and the boat ripped open. He'd called 911 but hadn't really connected.

"Thank God the people on another boat heard our screams and picked us up. One of them took care of Mom, and another contacted his yacht club." Shuddering as he recalled the scene, he tried to control the spasm in his throat. His hand trembled as lifted his coffee mug.

"Lord." Nora shook her head.

"An ambulance met and brought us here," Carter finished. "That's about it. Logan's getting his arm fixed so we can go home." He closed his eyes. "Can we just go home, Mom?"

"You bet, honey. As soon as the doctors say it's okay." She held him in her arms, while Dirk patted his knee.

Doug recovered his composure enough to let them know that David's friend, Dr. Strabowski, was going to check Logan and their mom.

"She—she won't be going home. At least not right

away." His voice cracked again. "We're just damn lucky–" He couldn't finish.

"But she's alive. And this Dr. What's-his-name'll take good care of her, right?" Dirk's face was gray as he spoke.

Doug gulped and nodded. Finally, when he was able to mouth a few words, he mumbled, "It's all my fault. Having to play the big shot with that damn boat–"

"Aw, Uncle Doug, we were having a great time!" Carter eyes peeked out from under his massive bandage. "And we'll do it again as soon as–"

"Not on that boat, buddy. Not on that boat." Doug leveled a sorrowful gaze at his nephew. "She's a goner."

Suddenly alert, Carter was eager to share the knowledge he'd gained from his sophomore econ class. "But there's that thing called insurance. You'll just buy another one—maybe even a better one. And we can all–" Desperately, he looked around for support. "We can all go out again."

"'Fraid not, Carter." Doug took a deep breath. "No insurance. No boat. No nuthin'."

"But our teacher said you're always supposed to get ins–"

Doug saw Dirk take a firm hold of Carter's arm and give him a stern look.

"Here comes a doctor now," Dirk interrupted.

A man in green scrubs pulled down his mask, revealing his weariness as he walked toward them. He bypassed them, however, and went straight to the family in the corner. His shoulders sagged as he took the mother's hands in his and whispered gently to her.

The immensity of the family's grief filled the room as

they reeled from his announcement.

"Mi bambino! O, mi bambino!" the mother wailed.

The father shook the doctor and rattled off something in Spanish.

When a chaplain emerged from the treatment area, he comforted them while the doctor rubbed his own head and tried to deal with the futility of it all.

Doug and his loved ones fell silent in respect. That poor family, he imagined, had probably gotten up that day and gone about their normal routines until they'd found themselves in the midst of this unspeakable tragedy.

There are some things, he thought, that are worse than losing a boat.

Doris

That Afternoon

"Faster! Faster!" From inside a head that seemed to be stuffed with cotton, Doris felt herself form the words.

She thought she could smell leaves burning as she, Rosie, Cheryl, and Kate tried to escape the hobos who were hot on their heels near the old train trestle. But the bikes they were pedaling were immersed in water and wouldn't move. She couldn't get her breath! Her friends were trapped! The hobos would get them! Again she tried to pedal.

"Help!" Panic-stricken, she jerked. "Help!"

"Hold still, Mom. You're gonna pull out your tubes."

Who was that? Sounded like Dougie.

"Gotta get away," she insisted. "Can't swim!"

"You're okay, " the voice reassured her. "You're okay."

Dougie? Was that really Dougie talking? What was <u>he</u> doing here with her seventh-grade friends? And what had happened to the girls? They seem to have vanished.

She opened one eye and was blinded by such a sea of white that it made her dizzy. Quickly, she closed it again and waited for the rolling sensation to stop. Someone must've doused the bonfire. She couldn't smell it anymore. Only that sharp too-clean smell of alcohol and hospital sheets.

A hospital? Yeah, that was it. Just had a baby girl, I bet. I'm gonna name her Darcy, she thought. When she opened her eyes again, she saw Bill. Or at least the guy looked like Bill. Damn him anyway. He'd gotten her pregnant again— only thing he was ever good for.

But this guy seemed different somehow. Worried, with a toothpick in his mouth. And the guy next to him looked a lot like him, only blond. Of course. She took a deep breath. Dougie. It <u>was</u> Dougie who'd spoken to her. And that other fellow must be Denny, always the spittin' image of his dad.

What were the two of them doing, watching her sleep after she'd just had a baby? Didn't they have work to do?

"She's wakin' up," she heard Denny say, and then suddenly there was Dirk-honey and Nora and that cute Polish girl Dougie had married. What was the whole family doing here—wherever <u>here</u> was?

"Hey, Mom." Dirk squeezed her hand.

God, she thought, he looks pale and awful. And all grown up. If that was Dirk and he was all grown up, she couldn't have just given birth to Darcy. She felt a dull ache in her arm as she rubbed her eyes with a bruised hand.

"What the hell?" Her own voice sounded fuzzy.

Throughout the rest of the day they fed her scraps of information until she fell asleep. She had no idea how long she'd dozed before they told her a bit more.

There'd been fog. She kinda remembered that. And the boat had hit something. As she recalled the frigid power of the waves beating on her, she faded out again.

When she wakened, a familiar square-built man with a reddish-brown beard and receding hairline had joined them.

"Hi, Mrs. Lochschmidt." His voice was warm and calm as he greeted her. "I'm Dr. Strabowski. Remember me? David's friend from Purdue. You brought us a picnic lunch one time. With great oatmeal raisin cookies." He smiled, revealing the signature gap between his two front teeth.

"You're not a doctor." She peered into his deep blue eyes. "You're—you're Suds!"

"Yep, you've got my name right. But—" He pulled up a chair and took her hands in his. "Guess what. I _am_ a doctor."

"Well, you've grown up then," she observed.

"That I have." He stroked his whiskers. "And guess what else. You broke bones in both your legs when that boat wrecked."

In protest, she tried to wiggle her legs. God almighty, she thought, they were like concrete blocks. She tried to absorb the news Suds had given her. Could he really be a doctor or was she dreaming? She willed her legs to move but felt no response.

"Both?" She swallowed. "Broken?"

Suddenly, she was consumed by the familiar anxiety that had always unsettled her as she walked by the spooky old Naughton mansion when she was growing up. Now, here she was again–right in the middle of a bad place–and wasn't sure how to handle it. She didn't have time for broken legs. She had parties to cater and a restaurant to run! Clamping her eyes, she tried to will away all that was happening to her.

The doctor spoke in soothing tones. Shit, she thought,

he really is Suds! Maybe she'd better call him "Dr. Suds" from now on. But what the hell had happened? A wrecked boat? Oh, yeah. There'd been all that water around her. Then Dougie's strong arms. She drew a deep breath and focused her feeble energy on the man talking to her.

"But I fix broken bones every day." Dr. Suds gave her such a look of endearment that she felt as if they were the only two people in the room. "And when I'm done, you'll be baking those good cookies again, better than ever." He patted her on her arm and turned to her family.

Through the gauze that enveloped her mind, she heard snippets of his conversation with her cluster of loved ones: "Already washed out the right leg with the complex fracture—lots of junk in there that we had to cleanse—probably do it again before we set the leg in three or four days—left one's not as bad—plate in it when we do the other one—rehab—six-to-eight weeks—lucky to be alive—I'll call David."

"You're sure you're old enough to be a doctor?" She thought her words sounded thick, like mountains of meringue piled on a lemon pie. She could feel herself drifting away again.

"Yep—but I still like cookies." He gazed earnestly into her face. "Maybe, after you're back to normal, you'll make me a batch. Deal?" The doctor—Suds–was moving toward the door. "In the meantime, I'll take good care of you."

"Deal." She forced herself to speak before the fatigue again swept her away.

When she awoke, the early evening sunlight filtering

through her blinds had softened the glare in her room. Nora was talking about taking Carter and Logan home. Oh my God, she thought. They'd been on the boat, too, hadn't they? When she asked, Dirk assured her the boys would be fine.

Breathing a sigh of relief, she reached for Dougie's hand.

"Thank God we'll all be okay. Sooner or later." When she closed her eyes, she could still feel the sloshing of the waves. "Dr. Suds'll do a good job."

Drowsily, she tried to reconstruct all that had happened since they'd roasted marshmallows on the boat. She recalled being tossed by the icy power of the waves when she'd tried in vain to paddle, She opened her eyes wide.

"Dougie!" she exclaimed.

"Yeah, Mom. I'm right here."

"Oh my God, Dougie, I just realized. If you hadn't been there to save me–" She could feel her breath coming in short, shallow puffs. Again she struggled for words. "Oh, Dougie, I'd have–I wouldn't have made it." She exhaled. "Thank you," she added weakly.

She wondered at the sudden stillness in the room. Nobody spoke. The silence was broken by the clatter of early supper trays and the gentle bubbling sounds in the tubes attached to her. Finally, when Dougie's fingers closed around hers, his hand felt strong yet cold as a corpse, and his face wore the same stunned expression he'd had when he'd broken a neighbor's window when he was ten.

"You're gonna make it, thank God," he told her seriously, then bit his lip. Hell, he looks nervous, she thought as she wondered what he'd been up to.

"But, Mom," he continued. "I've gotta tell you. It wasn't me. It wasn't me who saved you."

"Then who–"

"It was Denny, Mom. It was Denny."

Doug

September

He couldn't believe that Denny's old pickup was already parked in the dusty lot behind Rigoni's when he pulled in. The guy had never been on time for anything in his life. Now he was early.

It was just one more change that had come over Denny since the accident a few weeks ago. As he locked his car and headed toward the back door of the tavern, Doug recalled that his older brother had been decent, actually kind to their mom for the first time that he could remember. Denny'd gone to Rush to visit her twice while she was recuperating, then made the trip to the rehab in Danville three times every week. When Doug and Dirk had wondered who would stay with her when she came home after her six weeks in rehab, Denny'd volunteered.

"I'll do it." He'd shifted the toothpick in his mouth and held open the door to the lobby of the rehab center. They'd been too shocked to respond.

"Gotta sleep somewhere," Denny'd attempted a sheepish

smile. "I can do it as good as anyone else."

That sure had taken a load off their minds right then. Their mom, an emotional train wreck since the accident, seemed to get weepy at the tiniest thing. Just seeing Denny in her room brought tears to her eyes. Maybe, Doug thought, the two of them could patch things up after all these years.

Now, stepping out of the brilliant September afternoon sun into the familiar shadows of the tap room, he waited for his eyes to adjust before he spotted Denny seated at the bar.

"Hey, dude." Nick placed a mug of foamy draft next to Denny. "These are on me, guys."

Doug nodded as he settled himself on the barstool.

"That hasn't happened very often over the years," he chided his buddy. "What's the big deal?"

Nick was drying clean mugs with more energy than Doug had seen in a long time.

"Amy had her ultrasound this morning. A healthy boy." He slapped a hearty high five on Doug.

"Hey, that _is_ reason to celebrate, you old man." Doug felt Nick's contagious elation begin to spread. "A boy!" He echoed. "You lucky dude."

"Yeah—another Rigoni to continue the tradition." Nick could barely contain himself. "My grandpa started the business, so this one'll be the fourth generation."

"You sound like my dad." Denny spoke in a flat tone from his stool. "He was always prayin' for another boy, another farmer to help out with the work." He sipped his beer thoughtfully.

"Well," Doug tried to cover for his brother's lack of enthusiasm. "That's sure the best news we've had for a long time—the best since we heard that Mom can come home pretty soon."

Denny shifted uncomfortably. "Another?" he questioned, holding up his mug.

"You guys've been through a rough patch—your whole family." Nick shook his head as he filled Denny's mug to the brim.

Doug nodded silently.

"I heard the bank's taken over Dirk's greenhouse." Nick's features hardened. "That had to hurt—Priddy being his golf buddy and all. Has he got any work?"

"Not sure." Bracing himself, Doug suffered through another invitation from Nick to go out in his boat on Lake Vermilion. He'd had a hard time explaining to Nick that he wasn't in the mood.

"I mean—you've gotta get back out on the water and forget about the wreck." Polishing the bar, Nick uttered his tired old advice. Sometimes, Doug thought, his buddy didn't know when to put a cork in it. "And no insur–"

"Yeah, yeah. Back in a minute." Doug made a direct path to the men's room to avoid Nick's unsolicited patter. He still couldn't bring himself to talk about the "Windfall" with anyone but Maria. She'd been able to make him understand that his boat was "just stuff." But it still hurt like a kick in the groin to realize he might as well have dumped all of Alan's money into the lake.

When he returned, he drained his mug and held it up for a refill.

"We'll take spin in your boat before you put it away. That's a promise," he assured Nick. "I've just got a lot on my plate right now."

Nick gave him a thumbs up and turned to help other customers. Finally, Doug began to make small talk with his brother, covering the same old ground they'd worn thin since the accident.

First, they spoke again about how lucky they'd been that Denny'd been able to keep their mother afloat until the people in the nearby boat had rescued them.

"You're our hero, bro." Doug stared into his beer.

"She's my mom, too." Denny always gave the same answer.

Next, they talked about Dr. Strabowski and how he'd handled their mom's injuries so skillfully.

"Didn't hurt none that he was an old Polack, too." Denny repeated the remark he'd made several times recently. "When Mom remembered him from Purdue, she called him 'Suds.' Promised to bake him cookies."

"He sure went the extra mile for her." Doug grabbed a handful of pretzels and shoved the bowl in front of Denny. Pushing it aside, his brother declined. Strange, Doug thought. That wasn't like him.

"The whole thing still gives me nightmares," he confessed to Denny. "Thank God, Mom can come home in a few days. She oughtta be able to bear weight on her bad leg in a week or two." He washed down his pretzels with a swig of beer. "And thank God you're going to stay with her for awhile. I don't think she knows that yet, but she's gonna flip when she finds out."

Denny squirmed before he answered in a voice so soft that Doug had to strain to hear him. "That's why I wanted you to meet me today. So we could talk about that."

"I'm not sure which day she'll–"

"Oh, crap." Denny slammed down his mug. "I'm not gonna do it, Grumpy."

His words hit Doug so hard that he grabbed the bar.

"Whaddya mean—not gonna do it?" He could hear his reaction blasting over the din in the room. Hell, his insides were turning over.

"Just can't." Denny's reason was short and to the point. "I've got corn to get in pretty soon. I gotta be on the farm."

"But that's nothing new." He studied his brother. God, he thought, he looks the way I remember Dad when I was little—shoulders all hunched up before he'd let loose with a tirade that'd rattle the dishes in their cupboard. He shivered. "So," he probed, "something's changed. You mad at Mom again for leaving Dad?"

Denny shook his head.

"You like your old farmhouse better'n Mom's house?" he hammered away.

"Nope," Denny barely whispered. "Just the privacy."

"Privacy?" Doug exploded, then lowered his voice. "Why the hell do you need privacy?" He examined his brother's features. Then it hit him. "You got a new girl or something?"

"None of your business, Grumpy. I just can't do it."

Doug put his head in his hands, aware that Nick was warning them this would be their last freebie.

"I already talked with Darcy," Denny continued. "Her and the girls—mainly Mallory–will take care of Mom. She said it's no big deal."

"Shit." Doug's hand shook as he lifted his glass. Some things never change, he thought. And Denny was one of them.

"They'll do a better job 'n I could," Denny apologized. "But you're right about one thing." A grin played at the corner of his mouth. "I got a cute little nurse's aide from the rehab in Danville who's gonna move in with me."

Doug shook his head, then scolded himself as he questioned, who am I to judge? Before he met Maria, he'd been a lot like his oldest brother– a skirt-chaser with a temper he still fought to control.

"Well, at least you covered your bases." He patted Denny on the shoulder as he rose to leave. "And you'd better come around and see Mom three or four times a week."

"Yep." Denny whirled on his barstool and adjusted his Cargill cap. "Now that I'm finally gettin' to know her, I'm finding she's a tough old girl. With a good heart."

"And she bakes great cookies." Doug managed a smile. "Just ask Dr. Suds."

Dirk

September

"I think I'll make something for supper out of the rest of this rotisserie chicken."

Studying the contents of their refrigerator, Nora mused aloud to herself that she could throw in some veggies and put it all in a cream sauce over toast.

"Sounds good." Dirk started toward the back door. "We've still got some carrots in the garden that need to be dug up. I'll get 'em."

With the foreclosure on Redbud Hill just days behind them and money in the bank a scarce commodity, they welcomed any meal that the two of them could scrape together. He jumped as he opened the door, startled to find Barley standing on the step with his finger on the doorbell.

"Special delivery." Barley beamed as he handed Dirk a large insulated take-out bag filled with a piping-hot pizza.

"But I didn't order anything," he stammered. "Nora, did you–"

"She didn't either." Barley placed the container on their

kitchen table and unzipped it. "All your favorite toppings, my friend. Just the way you like it."

Stunned and touched, Dirk motioned for Barley to sit. He was thankful for Nora's gracious acceptance. Barley, he knew, was not high on her list of the folks she admired most in Rockwell.

"Can't stay," Barley answered. "It was kinda slow down at the store and I thought you all could use a pick-me-up about now." His eyes darted about the kitchen, then settled on a square of linoleum in front of him.

"Been a tough week," Dirk admitted. "But the boys'll sure be glad to see this when they get home—if there's any left. Carter decided to try working out with the basketball team, and Logan's getting a late start for cross country 'cause of his arm."

"Sure you can't stay for a bite?" Nora, Dirk realized, was doing her best to make Barley feel welcome.

Shaking his head, Barley insisted he had to leave. When he opened the door, Dirk stepped out with him.

"Rotten card you got dealt. Whole town feels bad about it." Barley's gaze flitted from his van to the garden and back to the van.

"Yep." Shoving his hands into his pockets, Dirk kicked a stone as the two inched their way across the driveway. A flock of robins heading south scattered from the grassy patch near the garden.

After a moment of awkward silence, Dirk could wait no longer. "What ever happened to you know—what's-her-name?" He hoped he appeared cool and casual.

For the first time, Barley looked straight at him.

"You can't fool me, my friend. Talking about Gina, right?" When he smirked, his little fox teeth glinted in the sun.

"Yeah. Gina." He tried to sound disinterested.

"You didn't hear?" Barley opened the door to his van.

"Guess not." Lord, he hoped she and Barley weren't engaged or something.

"Well, like Hawk Harrelson says on the Sox broadcasts, 'She gone.'"

Dirk felt Barley's eyes trained on him for a reaction. Offering a nonchalant shrug, he felt his insides churn.

"Gone. Like that." Barley snapped his fingers. "A salesman buddy of mine took a shine to her right away. Said he could train her as a rep and someday she could have her own territory. Guess she was bored with Ol' Barley's back room, so she picked up–lock, stock and barrel–and moved to an apartment down near Carbondale several days ago. Told me she's up for a new challenge and ready to live in a warmer climate." He climbed into his van.

Trying to digest all of Barley's news, Dirk remained speechless.

"'Course, if she's true to form, the climate'll be hot— wherever she's at!" Barley chuckled and revved his engine. He began to back out of the driveway, then called out.

"Oh–she said to tell you she liked working in the greenhouse and that you were okay. 'Just a little old-fashioned' was how she put it. I think it kinda freaked her out that you played your uncle's old music so much."

"Whatever." Dirk felt his face flush. "Hey, thanks for the pizza."

"Enjoy!" Spinning the gravel, Barley fired the van down the driveway and squealed his tires as he turned onto the street.

Nora had their places set when he stepped into the kitchen.

"Nice of him to think of us." Eyeing the pizza, she slid two slices onto her plate. "First time I've known him to do anything thoughtful. He's usually looking out for number one."

"Yeah, I'm not sure if he feels bad 'cause I lost the green-house or guilty 'cause his own business is doing okay." He helped himself to two slices. "Either way, it's not going to affect my appetite."

"That's 'cause you, Thomas, never cheated anyone in your life." She took a big bite and sighed. "Seems like old times. Just the two of us."

Shoot, he thought as he chewed a bite of sausage with Barley's special mix of cheeses, the guy may be a shady character, but he does make the best pizza. Maybe it just tastes extra good because Nora and I are eating in our own kitchen again. Together.

"I'm sorry the boys aren't here, but it's okay. I'm glad Logan's about ready to run again." He wished all of them could return to those days before the accident.

She nodded, adding, "And I think it's great that Carter's not spending so much time at McDonald's right now, though lord knows we could use the money."

"Well, you know I'm looking." He bristled at the thought of their financial fiasco.

"I didn't mean that," she interrupted. "Carter was thrilled

214

when Doug said he'd coach him on how to make the special Panczyk corner shot."

"Yeah. Doug's really okay, you know that? I mean—he's sure got his own troubles too." He transferred another slice to his plate.

They were quiet again for a few moments. As the cuckoo clock over the stove ticked away, he tried to form his thoughts into words. Finally, he spoke.

"You know something?" He studied the pattern of the tomatoes on his pizza. "We've all got troubles—I mean, Doug losing his boat and Mom getting so banged up. And me–" He paused, realizing he now had Nora's full attention. "I—I know I should feel suicidal or something about our business, but the weird thing is I don't. It's like I feel—well, calm." He looked into Nora's green eyes. "Almost relieved, if you can believe that."

She pushed a lock of hair from her forehead. "Me, too," she admitted.

"You?" He couldn't believe what he was hearing. "You're the only one who's been out there doing anything positive."

"Not in the way it really counts. I thought politics would be the answer—you know, campaigning to try to get a new person in the White House. But," he saw tears trickling down her cheeks, "what does any of it matter if you lose what you love most? Like your family? God, Thomas, we came so close to losing our boys." Her shoulders shook as sobs overtook her.

Dropping his pizza onto his plate, he went to her, took her in his arms, and led her from the table to the sofa in the living room. Holding her, he listened as she wept and apologized for not having been there when they needed her.

"I was so selfish," she admitted at last.

"And so was I." Drained from absorbing her emotional purge, Dirk reminded her that he'd always wanted his own thing, not someone else's. "And when I finally got it, I didn't know the difference between being a good manager and— well, a mean dictator. Mom accused me of being just like my dad on the farm—and that's no compliment, believe me."

Supper forgotten, they began to piece together their regrets. He felt encouraged when he saw her square her shoulders and declare, "I'm going to be a better wife and mother. But," she added ruefully, "I can't give up everything I've worked for either."

He nodded, grateful to see some of the old fire return to her eyes. "The campaign needs someone here in Rockwell. I could put in as much or as little time as I please. I might do that."

"Just until November?"

"Just until November. Then I hope to be around to see Carter play for the Boulders."

He smiled. "And I—I'll find something. Somewhere. I know I will." He wished he believed his own words.

"We'll both check around." Dabbing her face, she suggested, "Let's leave the pizza out on the table for the boys and run over to see your mom. She loves to have company in the evenings."

"She's doing better since she got home," he said. "There were a few times when she was in rehab that I was afraid she'd throw in the towel."

"Not your mom." Nora smiled. "Not our Grand-do!

S'pose she'd like some pizza?"

"Are you kidding?" He recoiled at the thought. "She never could stand Barley. She'd probably get sick. Still," he added, "it was a–"

"A nice thought," she finished.

As he kissed away her words, he felt himself shedding the stress that had shackled him for way too long. There they were–just Dirk and Nora—a bit battered but starting down a new path together.

Together. He liked the sound of that. And although he didn't have the vaguest idea where his next paycheck was coming from, he knew he and Nora would get through the next days. Together.

Doris

October

Hey it's me back among the living, Well just bearly. I got home two days ago from the rehab prison in Danville and hope I never see the likes of that place again. Darcy and Mallorys taking turns staying with me. Fixing my meals and helping me get around.

It feels funny to have someone wait on me. Ive always been the one who did that. Making meals for my brothers when Mom was working. Cleaning up tables at the truck-stop. And cooking cooking cooking for my kids and the whole town of Rockwell all these years. I cant wait to get back on my feet and bake a pie. Coconut cream. Thatll be it.

Its been 8 weeks since that dam boat sunk and almost killed us all. Wasnt nobodys fault really. The fog was so thick. Dougie couldnt see nuthin and hit the end of a steel pier. Real real hard. I dont remember it hardly. Just the water. All that water beatin on me and draggin me every which way. I was scared shitless. Thot I was gonna die.

But Denny pulled me out. Thats right. DENNY. The kid

218

whos given me so much grief over the years. I still cant get over it. Hes been nice and sweet to me ever since. So every time I get mad about getting hurt I think about Denny and wonder if maybe the wreck was a good thing after all.

Hes got some cute girl from the rehab living on the farm with him now and seems real happy. So maybe I can stop worrying about him and worry about Dougie and Dirk instead. Dougie didn't have insurance on the boat, so he lost everything Alan gave him. Ditto for Dirk. The bank took back his greenhouses and he's got no job and no business.

I wish I could help my kids more but right now I cant even help myself. One of Davids Purdue friends is a bone doctor & took good care of me at Rush. Hes even been able to see how Im doing from xrays that the rehabs sent him online. Dont ask me how. I only know its working. Dr Suds I call him. I cant pronounce his last name let alone spell it. Dr Suds tells me I can start to put weight on my bad leg next week. Im ready today.

Sorry I havent been in touch but I do want to thank you all for the pretty plant you sent me at the hospital. It made me laugh that it came from the Fearless Four and had a little hobo stuck in between the leaves. I took it to the rehab and now its home with me in the bedroom the kids fixed up for me in my living room. Still blooming and so pretty. I havent killed it yet. Ha ha!

My kids told me I should start one of those online things called a blog to tell everyone how Im doing. Good grief! I can email you all and the rest of the people I know can get their news from the Rockwell grapevine. Its easier and faster.

I should be moving around pretty good by the first week

in December. Im going to bake Dr. Suds some cookies and take them to him when I see him. One of the boys will drive me to his office.

After that I want the 4 of us to get together at my house before Christmas. You all pick the date and let me know. Ill be here. Im not going nowhere. My girls will just have to cater all the Christmas parties this year.

You know what? When I was lying in that hospital and the rehab Id think about the stuff the four of us used to do when we was growing up. Sometimes a nurse would look at me kinda funny when Id laugh about something. All by myself. Those sure were good times back then.

You all plan to come to my place in Dec. In the meantime please say a prayer for my Dougie and my Dirk. I don't know whats gonna happen to them and they sure need all the help they can get.

Best friends forever—Doris

Doug

November 1

"Hey, dude!"

He finished swishing his corner shot and tossed the ball to Carter before he acknowledged Nick. Although this Saturday afternoon was unusually balmy for the dreariest month of the year, he sensed it would be their last outdoor session at the park this fall. With hundreds of red and gold maple leaves skittering across the concrete, he knew he'd have to find an open gym for their next drill.

"Hey, yourself. What's up?" Jogging to the hot silver Corvette Nick had picked up recently, he admired his buddy's car but felt no envy. Hell, he was still glad to be driving his old Grand Prix.

"Maria said I'd find you here." Nick's black hair gleamed in the sunlight. Traces of silver at his temples hinted at his age. "Wanna take a ride?"

"You kiddin'?" He still hadn't been on the water since the accident and didn't feel like starting today. "I thought you'd put the boat in storage. Besides–"

"Not the boat, numbskull. It is in the marina." Nick shook his head woefully. "You haven't paid attention to much lately, have you? Climb in." He patted the black leather seat beside him. "I wanna show you something before I have to go to work. It'll only take ten or fifteen minutes."

"Let me clear it with Carter first." He motioned for his nephew to join him, then told him to keep practicing while he left with Nick.

"Keep working on your shot. And a hundred free throws. I want you to keep doing that every single day. Got it?"

"Yeah." Carter's tone was reluctant.

"I'm not messing with you. So many games are won or lost at the free throw line. You know that." He gave Carter an encouraging thump on the back. "That's one of the things Bobby Knight always stressed."

"Bobby Who?" Carter dribbled the ball as he asked.

"Uh, never mind. We'll be back soon." Sliding into the Corvette, he wondered if these cars were being built lower to the ground or if he needed to tone up.

"These kids," he complained. "Don't even know who Bobby Knight was. Or is. Where to?"

He loved the growl of the engine as they tooled across town—nice on the open road, but a little much for driving around Rockwell. He was surprised when Nick flew down the streets on the Sweet Briar side of town, then screeched to a sudden stop in front of a neglected stone bungalow with a ramshackle wing tacked to its side.

"Here we are." Nick opened the door and jumped out.

As he unfolded himself from the Corvette and glanced around the neighborhood, Doug recognized the house.

"This used to be that little grocery where Mom and Aunt Violet would send us for bologna or a loaf of bread at suppertime." He waded through the tangle of grass toward the leaning addition and peered through the window. "They always carried bubble gum with outdated baseball cards."

"Yep." Nick grinned. "Heck and Tootie's. One of the last great neighborhood mom-and-pop stores. That's been awhile though. Where've you been? They shut down their business but stayed in the house until they finally had to go to the nursing home."

"I guess I haven't been down this block for a long time," he admitted, surprised to see Nick take out a key and slide it into the front-door lock.

Swiping a cobweb from his face, Doug tried not to inhale the stale odor that crept from every corner of the front room. A mouse scampered across his shoes and slid through a crack under the baseboard. Even the autumn sunlight couldn't brighten the deserted space.

"Amy and me?" Nick studied the walls as he made his announcement. "We're gonna buy this place."

Hell, Doug thought, Nick's made some stupid investments over the years, but this might be his worst.

"Why?" was the only word he could muster.

That was all Nick needed. He and Amy loved the character of the house—the stone on the outside and its basic "good bones" on the inside. It had a nice yard, and the park across the street, where they'd spent so much time when they were growing up, would be a great place for their own kids.

"It's got a ton of potential," Nick finished. "But we're only going to buy it on one condition."

"What's that?" He knew it couldn't be money. Nick could have just about anything he wanted.

"Okay. Just keep an open mind. You hear?" Nick's voice was calm and encouraging, the tone he saved for disheartened customers who shared their secrets with him at the bar. "We want you to rehab it for us."

"Do what?" He wondered if his buddy had been sampling too many of his own products behind the bar.

Nick explained again, this time adding that he and Amy could build a showcase in the upscale subdivision on the outskirts of town, but they liked this house. For so many reasons.

Doug hoped his shudder wasn't visible. Taking on this project had even less appeal than riding in Nick's boat. He explored the rooms, evaluating the sagging cupboards. He'd have to gut the kitchen. Hell, he'd have to gut the whole place plus tear down the old grocery addition.

Still, look at that beautiful stone fireplace, he thought. With the right design—and he'd have to get Maria's input on that—it could become the focal point of a cozy living room that would have more character than any brand new place in a Longworth subdivision.

Pete Nolan might even wake up from his economy-induced stupor and get excited about having to order materials. Construction had been so slow lately that Atwater's was begging for work.

"This is where Amy and I wanna raise our family." Burying his hands in his pockets, Nick grew serious as he stared through a grimy window. "Could even be the next trendy place to live in Rockwell."

224

"Hell, I hope not," Doug answered. "But sure, I'll do it."

"You're gonna do <u>what</u>?"

His mom sounded like the woman he remembered when she bellowed her response from her wheelchair in her kitchen. Her spoon dangling in midair, Maria stopped stirring onions in his mom's big black skillet. Cherisse ignored him and continued chopping a cabbage.

He'd just dropped off Carter and thought he'd stop by to share his news with the women in his life.

"Hey, isn't she kinda young to be using that sharp knife?" The sight of his granddaughter wielding a weapon over cabbage wedges spread out on a wooden board made his heart stop.

Cherisse rolled her eyes. "I <u>am</u> almost ten, Gramps!" she reminded him, whacking the cabbage into smaller pieces.

"I was doin' that when I was eight—with nobody watchin' me," his mom stated. "We're keeping a close eye on her. Teachin' her how to make a big Polish dinner."

He took a deep breath of the simmering onions and potatoes bubbling in a pan.

"Smells fantastic." He poured himself a cup of coffee and sat down beside his mom.

"It's no big deal," he told them, relieved to see Maria recover enough to scoop Cherisse's cabbage into the skillet. "It's an opportunity, really."

As he explained Nick's plans for Heck and Tootie's, he realized he was operating on two different wave lengths.

While part of him poured forth Nick's amazing vision for a forgotten home in the depths of the Sweet Briar neighborhood, the other immersed itself in the family ritual he'd witnessed as long as he could remember.

After Maria added the paprika and tomatoes, his mom showed Cherisse how to place the kielbasa in the foil-lined pan.

"Man, that looks good!" Interrupting himself, he stopped to watch. Maria dumped in the cabbage mixture and arranged the potatoes around the kielbasa. All the while, his mom directed every step like Maria had never made a Polish dinner in her life,

He tried not to grin at Maria's extreme patience. They both understood that his mom's true recovery would not take place in the rehab center but in her own kitchen. After battling discouragement over her severe injuries and her depression when her "good leg" had to be reopened to clean out infection, his mom was starting to regain some of her old spunk. Making a Polish dinner could do that, he realized.

"I'll need your help." He studied Maria, always so pert when she was concentrating in the kitchen. "Nick and Amy are open for ideas on decorating—and that's your strong suit."

She slid the roaster into the oven and turned her full attention on him.

"I'd love to work with Amy." Her dimple deepened as she considered the idea. "We'll need to see your plans first, of course." She gave him that lingering gaze that always made him feel like the luckiest dude in the world. "You know," she reflected, "there might be more than one family that would like to buy an older Sweet Briar home and have you fix it up."

"Yep," he agreed absently as his mind wandered down the streets lined with neglected houses.

"Anything that's good for Sweet Briar's good with me." His mom's eyes lighted up. "How'd your practice go with Carter?"

"He's coming along. If he works at it, I think he can move up to starting five on the varsity." He watched as Cherisse dipped her hand into his mom's cookie jar. "Two are enough," he warned.

"He'd better practice 'cause this his last chance." Cherisse nibbled at her cookie. She stopped when she realized the room had grown silent and all eyes were on her. "Well, that's what the kids at school have been saying—that Carter's a senior and all."

"At least they're talking about something besides the election." Maria put the empty skillet in the sink and filled it with soapy water.

"You can say that again!" His mother wheeled herself over to the counter and refilled her cup. "I'm so da—darn tired of these commercials on TV."

"And Carter says they're <u>really</u> tired of hearing about it from their mom." Doug recalled his nephew's pained expression as he'd shared with him how much he hoped his family could get back to normal after Tuesday.

"She's hardly ever home." Again, Cherisse spouted the obvious. "That's what Jaden Corbett says at school, and his brother runs cross country with Logan."

"Well, I doubt if Jaden Corbett realizes Logan's mom

has a full-time job." Maria wiped the clean skillet, poured herself a cup of coffee, and joined them at the table. "Plus Nora's worked so hard on the campaign. And—and everything else."

"It's that everything else that's got me worried." His mom shook her head. "Poor Dirk's been like a lost soul lately. He's tryin' to coach Logan on his runnin' and fixin' up things around the house. But it's losin' his business that's really hit him hard."

"Uncle Dirk'll like going to the basketball games," Cherisse chirped.

"One thing for sure." Doug rinsed his cup and placed it in the drainer. "We all just gotta keep our ears open for some kind of work he could do until—well, until something better comes along." He sniffed the air again. "What time's that dinner gonna be ready?"

Dirk

November 17

He'd felt like this once before in his life and didn't like it. Studying the brick wall in the outer office of Luke's Landscaping near Danville, he recalled a day in kindergarten when he'd caught a playground swing across the bridge of his nose as he'd pushed Kari Crenshaw. He'd waited on a hard chair for the school nurse and counted the bricks on her office wall while he'd clamped his teacher's handkerchief against his spurting nose. He'd dreaded going into the inner office.

Now he heard the telltale sign of his gut groaning as similar misgivings consumed him. The only difference was that today he wasn't trying to plug a bad nosebleed and his shoes weren't dangling above the tile floor. He'd promised Nora that he'd "at least talk with Luke Fletcher and see what he had to offer." If anything.

When the office door opened, a guy emerged and stuck out his hand. "Luke Fletcher." Dirk couldn't have been more surprised. He knew Nora had great respect for this self-made businessman and that she'd soaked up Fletcher's energy and expertise as they'd toiled together on the campaign. But he'd expected a trim, Ivy-League type in a polo shirt with a customized logo—not a frumpy, bald, forty-something fellow who was two inches shorter than Dirk.

He tried not to snicker at the first thought that flitted across his mind: "I'm meeting Humpty Dumpty." However, when Fletcher produced a crisp handshake and drilled his penetrating blue eyes on him, Dirk knew immediately how wrong he'd been. He thanked Fletcher for his time and followed him into his office.

In stacatto-like phrases, Fletcher stated his case:

"Loved working with Nora. An angel. A real angel."

Dirk nodded.

"Going to Washington as part of the team." Fletcher paused, almost as if he were trying to convince himself that the president and Democratic National Committee might need his services. He allowed his attention to wander to the text that chimed on his cell phone.

"That's great–" Dirk began.

"Need someone I can rely on to manage the works when I'm gone. Politics," he waved his hand, "are temporary. For me, this business," he pounded his desk with his fist, "is for keeps. Got it?"

"Got–" Dirk tried to interject.

"Good. Then walk with me. You can see the place while I tell you what I need." He grabbed his cell, sprang from his swiveling chair with amazing agility, and motioned for Dirk to join him. "Hope you didn't wear good shoes."

Again, Dirk felt like an obedient child as he trailed after

this man in charge.

"Acres and acres of nursery stock. Right here." Ding! Fletcher lost a step while he glanced at another text. "Good supply of all kinds—shade, ornamental, about anything anyone would want. Raise our own."

In spite of his lumpy physique, Luke Fletcher moved with the speed of an Olympic athlete. Dirk hustled to keep up with him as they charged through rows of trees. Red leaves clung to wispy branches on young maples, while strong oaks still wore the coats of brown leaves that would blanket them through the winter.

"This section's just part of it. Can take the truck to one of the other fields." Fletcher whirled to retrace his steps, glancing at the new message on his screen. "Gotta show you one of the greenhouses."

Dirk caught his breath while Fletcher ticked off his needs:

"Someone who can run things while I'm gone. Pruning. Wrapping. That sort of thing.

"Someone who can tend the indoor plants and start the seedlings for spring.

"Someone who knows a little bookkeeping, who can track my figures while I'm gone."

He turned and fixed his remarkable gaze on Dirk.

"Someone who's not afraid to get his hands dirty."

Each requirement hit Dirk with the same force as Kari Crenshaw's playground swing. Before he could comprehend one of Fletcher's needs, another had nailed him. Trying to sift through all this successful man had tossed his way, Dirk stepped into the greenhouse and almost swooned when he inhaled the intoxicating odor of growing things. He excused himself to find a bathroom.

Inside the cubicle, he realized how shaky he felt—the same way he'd reacted when Ben had told him about his inheritance. He'd never considered the depth of his grief over his failure to keep Redbud Hill afloat until he'd entered this greenhouse and whiffed the sweet smell of new life. He splashed cold water on his face and washed his hands.

When he saw his reflection in the mirror, he knew he was hardly the picture of success. He'd thrown the dice, gotten what he'd thought he'd always wanted—and lost. Now here he was, back at square one, shackled with the responsibilities of debts and a family to support. He tried to don a positive air.

"Sorry about that," he apologized as he rejoined Fletcher.

Luke had picked up a hose and was spraying plants with one hand and conducting a phone conversation with the other. He confirmed an order for inauguration tickets, then turned to Dirk.

"Gotta keep these perennials healthy till spring." He finished one row and turned off the spigot. "Let's go back to my office."

Inside again, Dirk felt himself relax as he listened to Luke Fletcher spit out the condensed version of his road to success. A poor boy himself, he'd scraped together a few dimes to buy packages of seeds when he'd been in sixth grade. His garden patch had produced so much that he'd set up a stand and sold vegetables. By the time he graduated from high school, he owned a thriving business.

"Never got sidetracked with sports. Didn't have the

physique for it." Fletcher's wry smile indicated his appreciation of his own self-deprecating humor. "Only took a couple
of business courses at the junior college. Didn't have the
time to waste, so I learned the hard way." Again his eyes met
Dirk's with a look of understanding. "Nora says you've been
doing a bit of that yourself."

Dirk squirmed but kept his gaze locked on Fletcher.
Knowing he could trust this man who'd made his own way,
he began to share the joy and misery that Redbud Hill had
brought him.

"Tough times." Luke shook his head. "Could be you're
a better bookkeeper than a businessman. No shame in that."
He glanced at his cell, then went on to admit some of his
own failures. "I can raise money, but don't ask me to orga-
nize a company picnic. Just no good at that social stuff."

"You golf?" Dirk asked.

"Only when I have to." Fletcher squirmed as he fiddled
with his phone.

"Like to boat?" Suddenly, Dirk felt as if he were the one
conducting the interview.

"Never cared much for the water."

"What do you do in your down time? Besides getting
someone from Illinois elected president?" Dirk wondered if
this driven guy ever allowed himself a wasted moment.

"Music. Listen to music." Fletcher inspected the paper-
weight in the palm of his hand.

"Country? Rock?" Dirk tried to envision what Luke
Fletcher might put on his iPhone.

"No, no, no, no, no. None of that shit. Oops! Sorry."
Fletcher's eyes crinkled into slits when he grinned.

"Standards. Just old standards."

Dirk felt his mouth drop open. "You're kidding. I thought I was the only one who likes that stuff."

Luke's expression grew hopeful. "Big bands?" he asked.

"Some." Dirk no longer felt like the kid in the nurse's office. He relaxed against the back of his chair. "Mostly I like my uncle's old renditions on the piano. You may have heard of him. Tommy Panczyk."

For the first time that morning, Luke Fletcher was totally still. Ignoring two rapid-fire texts, he stared at Dirk in disbelief.

"Tommy Panczyk was <u>your</u> uncle?"

"Yep. My mom's brother."

Fletcher ran his hand over his bald head and turned off his cell. "I <u>love</u> his music. You have any of his old albums?"

"All of 'em. Wanna hear one sometime?"

"Well, yeah. Sooner the better." Luke sprang from his chair, his legendary verve obvious. "First, we need to talk about your pay. Won't be much right off the bat. Need to show you the ropes, then we'll see how it works out. Can you come at eight on Monday morning?"

"Sure—sure. I'll do my best for you." He could feel excitement building inside as he took a tiny step toward a new future.

"Know you will." Fletcher pumped his hand. "Have you got your uncle's album with 'Smoke Gets in Your Eyes'?" He smiled when Dirk nodded. "Bring it along. Okay?"

"Will do." As he stepped into the pale November sunshine and surveyed the acres of young trees he'd be tending, Dirk felt a blanket of peace settle over him.

"Wait'll I tell Mom that Fletcher's a die-hard fan of Uncle Tommy's," he thought.

Revving up his truck, he whistled "'S Wonderful"all the way home.

Epilogue

2008

Doris

Mid-December

"Look at this!" Kate's voice was full of awe, the way it used to be when she received a new autographed picture of Van Johnson. "It's one of those first editions of 'Rudolph!' Remember how much we all loved that story?" Reverently, she placed the yellowed book on the table in front of the living-room window.

"Tommy bought that for Mom with his own money," Doris recalled, steadying herself with her cane as she hobbled over to review her prized collection of holiday nostalgia or–as Dougie had labeled it when he'd been a teenager—her "holy crap." She studied the little tree with bubbling lights in the middle of the table.

"We musta been in eighth grade about that time," Rosie said. "'Cause I remember going up to Ward's with Colleen to get a copy for Mike and they were all sold out."

"I can't believe you still have some of Tommy's old sheet music." Cheryl picked up a copy of "Winter Wonderland" and began to hum a few bars.

"It's prob'ly some that your dad gave him, Kate." When Doris spoke to her old friend, she was stunned to see how thin Kate had become. Her hand-knit Christmas vest looked like a man's sweater draped over a kid's hanger. She knew Kate was worried sick about Marty and the progression of his Parkinson's, but could that be the only reason she was so damn skinny? She'd make sure Kate got plenty of calories today.

She'd felt like a kid herself all morning, waiting for an hour by the front window for her first glimpse of Rosie's car. Her friends had made a plan with more twists than a county-fair pretzel. Since Cheryl didn't drive anymore because of her macular degeneration, she'd taken the train to University Park. Kate had driven from South Bend to pick her up, and the two of them had gone on to Rosie's near Kankakee. There, they'd stopped for a potty break, then piled into Rosie's car for the drive to Rockwell. Oh my God, they must've wanted to come really bad. Squinting up her eyes so nobody could see the tears that threatened to roll down her cheeks, she motioned for all of them to make themselves comfortable.

"Mallory's fixin' our lunch in the kitchen," she explained. "Darcy's got a club party to cater, but that's okay. Mallory's been stayin' with me since—well, since last summer."

"Seems funny not to have Violet here to boss us around." Cheryl's hair swept her shoulders as she found a place on the couch. "She never could get over the fact that my mom brought me up on minced ham, white bread, and Grapette. Told me more than once she couldn't figure how I could belt out a song on a diet of 'that crummy plastic food,' as she used to call it."

"Is she doing okay?" Kate stationed herself stiffly on the edge of a straight-back chair. "I know she had to go to the nursing home–"

"Oh, she's doin' fine. In her own little la-la land." Doris tried to find the words to tell them that her sister had finally adjusted to life at "Almost Home," once the staff realized they needed to ask her each day what they should plan for dinner. Of course, Violet never remembered from one moment to the next, but somehow she believed, in her own foggy mind, that she was in charge. And she warned the workers every day not to let the gravy get lumpy.

"Wow—ee!" Rosie whistled softly. "That's the biggest tree I've ever seen in this room!"

"And it's real." Cheryl let the branches tickle her nose as she inhaled the fragrance of the soft needles.

"Know where that came from?" Doris let her gaze wander away from her friends to the towering white pine that spilled out of the corner of the room.

"Not the Piggly Wiggly. That's for sure." Rosie clamped her mouth firmly.

"Denny brought it," Doris told them. "Cut it down and brought it in from his farm. Crazy thing hung clear out the end of his pickup." She dabbed her cheeks with a tissue, wondering if the blast of cold air that had come in with the girls was making her eyes water.

"Denny?" the three chimed in unison.

"You got it." She was relieved to see Mallory beckon from the kitchen door. "I'll tell you more after lunch. Hey, c'mon. Everything's ready."

"Need help?" Cheryl stepped up, offering her arm.

"Naw, that's okay. I just have to rock back and forth to get up a head of steam so I can get out of my chair."

As she led her friends into the spacious kitchen, Doris thanked her lucky stars once again that Violet and Spud had been smart enough to pick out this house with big rooms. She rejected that nasty little mental invitation that urged her to speculate what would have happened if they hadn't bought a house that could hold her and the six kids when Bill had become so doggone mean. Asking herself that question was like wandering into a dark, scary alley filled with bogeymen. No way was she going there. And certainly not today!

"Mallory, you've done yourself proud." She stopped to consider the well-set table with its holiday place mats, centerpiece of holly sprigs, and homemade cranberry salad with dollops of cream in the little Christmas bowls Alan had given her a few years ago. "My friends never had it this good back in my house when we was growin' up. They helped me cut dandelion greens and fry pork steak."

"Well, they won't have to do that today." Mallory's gray eyes twinkled as she spoke. "Hope you're not all disappointed."

Doris beamed as she watched her granddaughter, decked out in her red shirt and Santa Claus apron, chat easily with her old friends. My God, she thought, Mallory looks so much like me when I was her age, but I had six kids by then and she's just makin' wedding plans.

"This is Grandma's old standby, but it's what everyone in Rockwell wants for their Christmas luncheons." Mallory set plates with scoops of scalloped chicken and crisp green beans in front of each guest. "The dinner rolls are on the table. Oh, and don't forget to save room for her traditional chocolate peppermint dessert."

"I woulda made pie, but it's still kinda hard for me to roll out a decent crust," Doris apologized.

As her friends attacked their lunch, they fell into comfortable conversation. When Kate asked about the accident, Doris began, "Well–" and shook her head. "After we're done eatin'." She was grateful to hear Cheryl ease into another topic.

"I was so sorry I wasn't in the city when you were in the hospital. I'd gone to Boston with a group of board members from Children's Memorial for a conference." Her brown eyes shone as she tasted a bite of cranberry salad. "I loved hearing how we can make a child's stay in the hospital more pleasant—and Boston's an amazing city."

After Cheryl had described the historical places she'd visited and the incredible seafood she'd devoured, Kate mentioned that Marty had always enjoyed covering the Boston College/Notre Dame game for *The South Bend Tribune*. When Doris asked about Marty, she was almost sorry she'd put Kate on the spot.

"His illness is progressing." Kate twitched slightly as she nibbled at the edge of a roll. "But he's where he should be. In the extended-care wing." Staring at her plate, she continued, "I'm glad I'm close by. You're right, Cheryl. Assisted living can be a pretty great thing. I see him every day and am making new friends there."

"Some days I've got more assistance than I want—right in my own house," Rosie grumped. "The health care people

242

must be making a mint off all the oxygen tanks they're dropping off. But I do need 'em. Fried fritters! Why didn't someone tell me if you smoke like a stovepipe when you're young, you'll be dragging around metal canisters when you're old?" She slathered soft butter on a second roll and took a healthy chomp.

"You just never listened." Doris couldn't resist chiding her old friend.

"None of us listened." Cheryl ran her fork around her plate to capture the last bit of casserole. "I didn't. Did any of you?"

"Not much. I felt my folks didn't know anything." Kate's breath seemed to come in little puffs. "Back in seventh and eighth grade I only listened to all of you!"

"Sometimes," Doris fumbled for the right words, "when I think back on who I was, I—well, I can't believe it was me. Does that make any sense?"

Nodding in agreement, they fell into their habit of recounting old times while they ate their dessert. When they adjourned to the living room, Doris used her cane to poke around the stack of tapes under the library table.

"Mallory, would you put in that Christmas tape of Tommy's? That one right there." She brushed over an old cassette case that bore Tommy's picture. "Good thing we still have a cassette player," she added. "Most people seem to listen to music on their phones these days."

With her brother's piano rendition of "Do You Hear What I Hear?" filling the room, she settled herself on the sofa. Being with these old friends was the best medicine she'd had since—well, since. Taking a deep breath, she decided to

243

begin her tale.

"Okay, you guys. You've all been wonderin' what happened that night. Me, too, in a way." She glanced first at Rosie, then at Kate and Cheryl. She had their full attention. "I only know one thing for sure. It wasn't Dougie's fault."

Closing her eyes as she let Tommy's soothing strains of "O, Tannenbaum" calm her, she allowed herself to return to the summer scenes she'd tried to erase from her memory. Softly, almost to herself, she recounted their evening on the boat—Denny's surprise appearance, Carter and Logan's joy at taking the wheel, the taste of toasted marshmallows, the fun they'd shared as the "Windfall" sloshed through the waves. Even now, she could feel the wind in her face and the terrible jolt that pitched her onto the floor as the boat tossed, struggled, and began to break up. Once again, she was overwhelmed by the power of the water. She paused as she remembered the pain, that excruciating pain in her legs. And the fear, the knowledge that this was it for her. Even today, she could still take comfort in the strength of the arms that wrapped around her and the voice that assured her, "I've got you, Mom."

She realized tears were streaming down her cheeks and let them go unchecked.

"I thought it was Dougie. I thought sure it was Dougie." Closing her eyes again, she continued. "I didn't know a thing till I woke up in the hospital with half the world around my bed. That's when I found out it was Denny who'd saved me."

No one uttered a word for several seconds.

"Wow!" Cheryl murmured. "When you told us that in your email, I couldn't believe it."

"It's a miracle—one of the best Christmas stories I've ever heard." With effort, Kate rose to give Doris a hug.

"Oh, my God, you need to put meat on those bones." Doris tried to cover her shock at Kate's fragile physique.

"I'm working on it. Going to see my cardiologist next week," Kate added as she returned to her chair. "I haven't had my usual pep lately."

"Maybe you need some of what I've got." Rosie fingered her silver oxygen canister. "I don't leave home without it. Colton says some artist could make a bundle if he'd paint some funky designs on these things. You know, give 'em some flair."

"Great idea!" Cheryl jumped on the idea. "Think what that would do for morale in the hospitals."

"So," Kate urged. "Back to the hospital."

"Yeah. Scary places if you ask me." Doris resumed her tale. "If it hadn't been for Dr. Suds—oh, my God, I have to tell you all about him."

She felt her energy returning as she spoke of how David's old college friend had cared for her and how she'd have to keep him in a lifetime supply of cookies to show her appreciation.

"David and his family are coming, you know—for Christmas. First time in years." She still couldn't wrap her mind around the fact that all six of her kids would be with her. Oh, how she wished she could return the greenhouse to Dirk and restore the "Windfall" for Dougie this Christmas. She winced, thinking of how her boys had accepted Alan's

245

generosity and lost it all in three short years.

"You cold, Grandma?" Mallory brought in a tray of hot coffee. "I could turn up the heat."

"Thinkin'. Just thinkin'." God, how she loved this grand-daughter. "That makes me shiver sometimes. Shouldn't do it, I guess."

"Thinking about what, hon? Spill it all out." Cheryl gave her a sympathetic look. She'd always been good at that, Doris recalled. "After all, you <u>are</u> among friends."

Little by little, she began to stammer out her concerns about Doug and Dirk and all the problems their inheritance had brought them.

"I wish Alan had told me what he was plannin' to do," she said. "I would've told him to give his money to the town park or something. Someplace where it would've done some good."

"Maybe it did do some good." Kate frowned thought-fully and placed her cup on her saucer.

"Yeah," Rosie echoed. "Your boys were able to get what they'd wanted all their lives. Nothing wrong with that."

"No." Doris set her cup on the end table. Staring at the nostalgic ornaments on her huge tree, she felt a realization begin to dawn on her. "They both got what they <u>thought</u> they wanted."

"Did they enjoy what they had?" Kate leaned forward, her intensity returning.

"Yeah." She recalled the first two years and how her sons had thrived. "But then everything seemed to get turned bass-ackwards, if you know what I mean."

"Like?" Cheryl's question hung in the air.

"Like the business I thought was the perfect investment for Dirk went sour. His family suffered and–" She let her voice trail off as she thought of Nora's defection, Gina's wacky charms, and Dirk's inability to manage. "Someday, I'll get you to help me write a book about all of it, Kate. I never dreamed it could all turn to shit for him."

"Guess he found out he's better off working for somebody else than trying to run the whole show." Rosie set her jaw to announce she knew she was right.

"And Dougie, God bless him, blew all his money on that boat." As Tommy's "O, Holy Night" blanketed the room with its peaceful strains, Doris could feel her eyes filling with tears.

"I don't know what's the matter with me," she apologized. "I haven't been able to stop crying since—"

"But did he enjoy it?" Kate repeated her question. "Did he love <u>having</u> that boat?"

Doris let her shoulders droop.

"Yeah, he really did. Took half the town for rides. Him and Maria spent a bundle on food and gas and maintenance. I think though–" Again, she recalled the strained look around Dougie's mouth last summer when he complained that people he hardly knew seemed to <u>expect</u> a weekend trip. "I think the newness had wore off and he was startin' to feel kinda used and abused by the whole thing."

"But, let me get this," Cheryl seemed bent on following this line of thought. "If Doug hadn't had the boat, he wouldn't have invited Denny. Right?"

"That's for sure," Doris agreed.

"And if Denny hadn't been on the boat, he couldn't have

been there to save you. And now the two of you have made up. And," she clasped her hands joyfully, "you've got your son back."

"Weird," Rosie stated. "This is just plain weird."

Doris stood, leaned on her cane, and began to take small steps around the room as she tried to process this revelation.

Could it be? Alan's money had taken her boys down a twisted path filled with both joy and heartache.

"You don't s'pose, deep down, Alan knew what he was doin', do you?" Doris leaned on her cane and peered at each of her friends. "I mean, he couldn't have known his money was goin' to bring me 'n Denny back together someday. He just couldn't have!"

"But your boys—are they doing okay now?" Kate persisted.

"Not too bad. No, not too bad at all." Glancing out the window at her barren lawn, she heard Tommy playing "The First Snowfall of the Winter" and hoped that's what they'd get for Christmas.

"Nora knows she's gotta stay closer to home. She even talked to one of her friends about a job for Dirk in Danville. At a big nursery." She felt a smile break across her face. "I think it might work out."

"And Doug?" Kate wondered.

"Well, for starters, he learned a lot. Like he should've had insurance on the boat." She fondled a papier mache ornament Cherisse had made last Christmas. "Now him and Maria are scraping their money together to get enough to adopt Cherisse. She's at their house all the time anyway, and Renee's movin' to Oregon with that Brandon guy she's been with for a year or so—says she wants to make a fresh start."

She paused, staring at a straggly old ornament that she'd salvaged from her own family tree.

"It's kinda like when my sister, Lorene, took off. Remember that?"

"Like it was yesterday," Cheryl said.

"But at least <u>she</u> finally came back for her kids," Rosie reminded them.

"That about killed my mom, but it all worked out. This will, too." Doris paused to consider the situation. "I've got some of Alan's money, too. And I'm gonna help 'em some with the adoption—kinda an investment in family, you know. That kid's so much like me that they call her 'Little Doris.'" She grinned. "Kinda freaky, huh?"

She went on to tell them that Dougie was going to rehab an old home and hoped to do more.

"That's a word we've been hearing a lot around here lately," she added. "Rehab."

"But it's doing wonders for you, Grandma." Mallory smiled and filled their cups with steaming hazelnut decaf. "Good thing, too. We need you down at The Boulder."

"Yeah, the infection that came on set me back, but I'm full speed ahead now. Actually, it was Denny who built that ramp out front when I came home." She savored the satisfaction of knowing she was on good terms with each one of her kids. At last. Alan would be so pleased.

"I think—I really think the boys'll be okay. In spite of the money and everything that happened." She paused as she searched the faces of her dear friends. "And I'm only going to say one more thing about all that. Then we can talk about fun stuff."

"What's that?" Rosie, of course, was the first to ask.

"I'm damned if I'm ever going to set foot in <u>anyone's</u> boat again!"

CPSIA information can be obtained at www.ICGtesting.com
Printed in the USA
LVOW06s2103300914

406629LV00001B/26/P